Chapter 1

A silk slip flew through the air and landed on my head. Pushing the soft fabric out of my face, I turned to stare at my maid who stood, hands on hips, glaring at me in a ferocious manner.

"M'lady, you are going to be late!" And apparently Maddie was having none of it.

Her foot tapped against the wood floor in an imperious manner. Really, if she'd worked for anyone but me, she'd have been sacked by now. She was dreadfully bossy.

"It's just Varant," I said, calmly removing the slip and inspecting my wave to make sure she hadn't knocked anything askew. Miraculously she hadn't, so I focused on swiping on lipstick. It was a new shade for me: pale rose. I wasn't sure I liked it, but it did go rather well with my dress, newly arrived from Paris. The Madeleine Vionette was a dream of silk georgette which floated around my curvaceous figure in a surprisingly elegant way.

"Just Varant?" she squawked, cheeks pink, eyes bulging. "He ain't a 'just' anything. He's a *Lord*."

As if that settled the matter. And I suppose it should have. We were the perfect match, at least on paper. Lord Peter Varant was of the upper classes and almost as rich as I was. He had admired me since probably the first moment we met, though I was still married at the time. He was also surprisingly enlightened for a man. And yet...

I sighed. "You're right, of course. I *should* be more excited. Unfortunately, I find myself able to manage it."

Maddie snorted.

Fortunately, the man himself chose that moment to ring the bell, saving me from more of my maid's remonstrations. After throwing me a final rather tart look,

Lady Rample and Cupid's Kiss

Lady Rample Mysteries – Book Six

Shéa MacLeod

Lady Rample and Cupid's Kiss
Lady Rample Mysteries – Book Six
COPYRIGHT © 2019 by Shéa MacLeod
All rights reserved.
Printed in the United States of America.

Cover Art by Amanda Kelsey of Razzle Dazzle Designs
Editing by Alin Silverwood

The characters and events portrayed in this book are fictitious. Any similarity to real persons, living or dead, is coincidental and not intended by the author.

No part of this book may be reproduced, or stored in a retrieval system, or transmitted in any form or by any means, electronic, mechanical, photocopying, recording, or otherwise, without express written permission of the publisher.

Shéa MacLeod

she marched her narrow behind out my bedroom door and down the stairs to let him in.

Heaving a sigh, I stared into the mirror, ensuring everything was in place and pretending I wasn't wishing that tonight's escort was someone else entirely. I knew I was being a ninny. It was over with Hale and me. He'd married someone else. Nothing to do but move on.

Squaring my shoulders, I rose from the vanity, grabbing my bag and wrap on the way to greet my date. The smile on my face may have been plastered on, but one would never know to look at me.

My name is Ophelia, Lady Rample. I'm considered by most to be a merry widow with too much money and not enough consideration for the gravity of my station. My natural curiosity—or perhaps suspicion—had led me to solve the odd crime on more than one occasion.

Varant greeted me in the foyer, my coat out and ready for me. "Good evening, Ophelia. You're looking lovely."

"Thank you. As are you." And he was. Varant was the sort of man every girl dreams of: tall, dark, handsome, and virile. He cut quite the figure in his dark dinner jacket and matching trousers, dark hair—lightly peppered with silver—perfectly pomaded. Yes, every inch the gentleman.

He helped me on with my coat, then ushered me out the door and to his waiting Bentley, which he drove himself. He wasn't one to waste money, and chauffeurs were a waste of money as far as he was concerned. Which was a shame, really. There were probably loads of men who could have used such a job, what with the economy the way it was. Not that I was one to talk. I much preferred to drive myself. More fun.

It was a chill night, and the air held an edge of ice. Dirty snow still lingered along the curb, though the streets themselves were clear. The weak light of the streetlamps cast eerie shadows, turning simple, barren tree branches into daunting witches' fingers.

January was never my favorite month. The holidays were over, taking with them their numerous parties and cheerful atmosphere. Spring had yet to peek from beneath snow banks. It was that gloomy in-the-middle time, and my mood matched it perfectly.

I refused to consider that my mood could be in part because the man currently sitting next to me in the motorcar was not the man I wished was sitting there. Naturally I told myself not to be a dumb Dora. That boat had sailed. Alas, I wasn't particularly listening to myself.

What I needed was a distraction. I just wasn't sure Varant would be up to the task. A good murder. Yes, that's what I needed. Unfortunately—or perhaps fortunately for the victims—murders weren't exactly thick on the ground at present.

"You seem to be in deep thought this evening." Varant's voice interrupted my thoughts. He'd a nice voice, posh accent and all, but it wasn't that rich, low rumble with the American twang I liked so very much.

"Just reflecting upon the season," I said with forced cheer. "Spring is just around the corner."

"Spring is at least two months away," he said dryly.

"Don't rain on my parade." I gave a light laugh that sounded false even to my ears. "Now, tell me, what have we got planned for tonight?"

"It's a surprise. I think you'll like it."

I lifted a brow but didn't press him further. I knew from experience he wouldn't say another word, and nothing I could say or do would convince him otherwise.

Eventually, the car pulled up to the curb next to a plain brick building on Wardour Street. It had started drizzling, and a doorman with an umbrella dashed over to help me out of the Bentley. Varant joined me under the striped awning, shaking water drops from his overcoat.

"I hope you like this place. It's new." He held open the door for me before the poor doorman had a chance.

Inside, the foyer was covered in a thick carpet of red swirled with black. The walls were papered in cream with a gold geometric pattern which matched the chandelier hanging above. A young man in the black-and-white uniform of the waitstaff appeared as if from nowhere to take our coats. An older man in the same uniform arrived to show us to our seats.

He led us through a pair of massive double doors inlaid with brass lions in the Art Deco style. Before us was a wide set of carpeted stairs leading down to a large room, also carpeted except for the wooden dance floor near the stage which sat at one end. A huge crystal chandelier hung from the center of the ceiling, dripping with faceted clear and red crystals the size of my fist. Below it spread dozens of intimate tables set for two, and huddled against the walls were cozy velvet upholstered booths that could handle up to four people.

The stage had been set up for a band with a black grand piano and stands for sheet music, but it was currently occupied by a single harpist. The middle-aged woman was dressed in a simple, dark blue evening gown and played with a great deal of panache.

We were led down the stairs to one of the booths near the front with a good view of the stage, particularly the piano. Once seated, Varant ordered drinks before I could so much as open my mouth. Something which irritated me no end. He hadn't even asked what I'd prefer. Nor had I heard him over the music. I shot him a glare, which he ignored with his usual aplomb.

I wanted to berate him, but the music was so lovely, I watched the musician instead. I could see why Varant would bring me to such a place. It was sophisticated and elegant, just like him. It was not, however, my sort of place. I preferred jazz clubs and speakeasies, low class as that might be.

The waiter returned almost immediately with a silver tray upon which sat two filled glasses. I lifted an eyebrow as he sat the drinks in front of us. "Old Fashioneds?" I do love my whiskey, as Varant knew, but I didn't drink Old Fashioneds customarily.

"Boulevardiers. Much more interesting," he assured me.

I took a sip. It was indeed intriguing, if not particularly to my taste. The flavor was rich and slightly sweet, but with the odd herbal tang of Campari which ruined it for me. "Thank you." What else was there to say?

"I hope you will approve of the rest of the evening as well," he said, though I'd never claimed to approve of his cocktail selection. His tone was meaningful. I took his hint but ignored it. I wasn't sure I was ready for that just yet. Not with him, at any rate.

The harpist finished her song, took a bow, and exited the stage, her place taken by what I could only assume was a Master of Ceremonies. He bowed slightly. "Ladies and Gentlemen. Welcome to The Lion Club. I hope you all have a most pleasant evening. And now, for our main entertainment. Hale Davis and his band."

I froze, glass half-way to my lips. Hale was here? I took a deep gulp of my drink, feeling the burn all the way to my stomach where the warmth spread out, easing my sudden discomfort. Had Varant known?

"Didn't know he was playing," Varant muttered. Although his expression remained completely calm, there was a tightening of the skin around his eyes. It was so slight, I would have missed it if I wasn't eyeing him so closely.

I guess that settled the matter. He hadn't known. And it didn't look like he was happy about it. Had he guessed I still carried a torch for my former love?

Five men strolled onto the stage, four black and one white. They took up their positions at various instruments, Hale taking a seat at the piano. It had been months since I'd seen him last. He looked...good. His suit fit him perfectly, showing off broad shoulders and a nipped-in waist. His hair was cropped close and carefully oiled, shoes shined within an inch of their lives. His dark skin glowed against the white of his shirt. My heartrate kicked up a notch.

His supple fingers danced over the keys, trilling out a series of sweet notes before plunging into one of the popular jazz songs of the year. I recognized it as *New Orleans* written by Hoagy Carmichael. It had a nice feel to it, but I couldn't focus on the music. I could only focus on Hale.

Hale Davis was my former paramour, for lack of a better word. We'd met at a jazz club where he was playing, and one thing had led to another. Perhaps it wouldn't have gone as far as it did if one of the club owners hadn't been murdered and Hale's band mates hadn't been accused of the crime. But our relationship had unfurled even as the investigation had and, between one thing and another, we'd had a very happy few months together.

Until some woman had shown up claiming he was the father of her unborn child, and he'd gone off to do the noble thing. I had almost convinced myself I was over him.

I knew the moment he spotted me. There wasn't even a fraction of hesitation in his music, but his eyes bored into mine, burrowing holes all the way to my soul. I jerked my attention away, focusing on my drink. Suddenly aware I was sharing my booth with another man.

Varant heaved a sigh. "You'll never be over him, will you?"

To that I had no answer.

"We can leave if you like."

I shook my head. I didn't want Hale to think he'd broken my heart. He hadn't. Although it had come close. He still might, if I let him.

As the evening progressed, I began to feel a nice, heady buzz. "Come, darling," I said, holding out my hand to Varant. "Dance with me."

He gave me an indulgent smile and took my hand, leading me to the floor where several other couples danced.

He took up a position dead center, naturally, making sure that Hale saw us together. Part of me felt a little thrill that Varant was so surprisingly territorial, and part of me was irked about it. I was no one's plaything.

But perhaps Varant didn't realize what he'd done. Or perhaps I hadn't given him enough credit. For he'd situated in just the right spot, so I could get a clear view of Hale, who never took his eyes off me through the entire song.

What did it mean?

It didn't mean anything. He was a married man now and had no business giving me google eyes.

The song came to a close, and the Master of Ceremonies appeared to announce the intermission. Hale didn't even wait for him to finish but sprang off the stage and strode toward me. He was barely ten feet away when a woman screeched, "There you are! Is that your whore?"

The entire restaurant turned to stare at the woman stomping across the carpeted floor. Her skin was a warm, pale beige, barely darker than my own, and her dark brown hair was done up in tidy waves under her cheap russet hat. She wore a matching coat, well worn, over a printed cotton day dress, far too light for the season. Her shoes, too, were scuffed and worn, though obviously they'd been cleaned and polished regularly.

She definitely didn't belong here, but she marched straight up to Hale and thrust herself between us. "Is this her?" she demanded, pointing quite rudely at me, her voice shrill enough to call the neighborhood dogs.

Hale took her arm and tried gently to steer her away. "Dottie, this is neither the time nor the place. I'm working."

She snorted, turning up her pert nose at me, hazel eyes snapping with fire. "Working, my ass."

An older woman dripping in diamonds gasped and teetered on a swoon. I thought her reaction a bit much, but Dottie's behavior *was* shocking.

"Excuse me, Lord Varant, Lady Rample, my wife isn't feeling well." The dark stains on Hale's cheeks spoke to his embarrassment and anger.

"Oh, lords and ladies, is it? Well, la di da. No time for your own *wife*." Her tone was an ugly snarl and her expression one to match.

I did not envy Hale having to live with this ghastly woman. But he'd made his bed. Both literally and figuratively.

He dragged her toward one of the doors which I could only assume led backstage, Dottie struggling all the way. Before he could force her through, she tore herself out of his grasp and ran at me, hands curled into claws. I stared, stunned. Her behavior was so beyond the pale, I could hardly register it. Fortunately, Varant remained alert

Before Dottie could rake her nails across my face, Varant picked me up bodily and swung me out of the way. The entire restaurant gasped. The Master of Ceremonies bustled over, two large men in tow. Between them, they wrestled the angry, spitting Dottie into submission.

"I think we should get out of here," Varant said, guiding me gently toward the stairs. "The evening seems to have soured."

I agreed wholeheartedly. If I never saw Dottie Davis again, it would be too soon.

Shéa MacLeod

Chapter 2

The next morning dawned, one of those gloomy, gray days that are inevitable during a London winter. Bitter cold wind whipped at the window sashes and whistled down chimneys. Maddie had lit a fire in the smallest sitting room so it was nice and cozy, and I decided to break my fast there, looking out over the garden—such as it was.

It was really more of a paved patio, hardly bigger than a postage stamp. Against the ivy-covered back wall was a small water fountain, turned off for winter. To either side were large, ceramic pots filled with barren plants. The furniture had been folded, covered, and tucked to one side.

The bare branches of my neighbor's alder buckthorn rattled and scratched together in the wind. Admittedly, the scene was rather bleak. Not unlike my state of mind.

I'd come to terms with Hale's marriage, or so I thought. He'd every right to make the choice he had. I understood it. The woman had been pregnant with his child, though she was obviously not pregnant now. She'd likely had the baby already. But he hadn't wanted his child to grow up without a father, and I respected that.

Still, the fact that such an intelligent, talented, kind man was saddled to such an inelegant harpy grated.

What grated even more was that he'd chosen *her* over me. Even though the real choice he'd made had been in favor of his child. The petulant part of me didn't like the logic.

"Stop this nonsense," I muttered into my cooling cup of coffee. "You need to move on. He has." Had he though?

"You alright, m'lady?" Maddie popped her head into the room. Her mob cap was askew, and she held a feather duster in one hand.

"I'm fine, Maddie," I said, pretending she hadn't caught me talking to myself. "What's on the agenda for today?"

She frowned and shoved her cap, which was listing over one eye. "Don't know about you, but I've got dusting to do." She shook the duster which sent a cloud of dust into her face. She let out a massive sneeze.

"Bless you," I said dryly.

She glared at the offending duster. "Guess I better get back to it. Unless you need anything?" Her expression told me that I better not need anything.

"I'm fine, Maddie. I've everything I need."

She sniffed and exited the room, letting the door swing shut with a bang behind her. The girl had a way of grounding a person.

Just then, the front door bell jangled. I could hear Maddie's footsteps marching down the hall, the front door opened, and then a murmur of voices. A short while later, my aunt sailed into the room, breath puffing as if she'd walked ten miles and cheeks flushed with the cold.

Aunt Butty was a woman of a certain age. She would never admit what age, but it was somewhere past sixty. She had a penchant for strong colors and bafflingly large hats.

Today was no exception. She wore a wool day dress of persimmon—the height of fashion for winter of 1933—with a silk scarf of vermillion and periwinkle. It was...startling to say the least.

Her cloche hat, however, was the *piece de resistance*. It was made of bright-green velvet with a rose-colored silk ribbon wrapped around and fastened in a rosette the size of a dinner plate.

I blinked in an attempt to adjust to the riot of color. It was a useless endeavor. "Good morning, Aunt Butty. Would you like a bite to eat? Coffee, perhaps?"

"Coffee, dear. And perhaps some of that toast with preserves. I'm famished. You will never guess what I just heard."

I eyed her over the coffee pot as I poured her a cup. "I give in. What did you hear?"

She took the proffered cup, swallowed a fortifying sip, then said, "Dottie Davis is dead."

I stared at her. "Excuse me?"

"You know," she said, busying herself spreading butter on several pieces of toast, "that woman Hale Davis married. The one who said she was pregnant. I have always had my doubts about that. Very convenient if you ask me—"

"Aunt!" I interrupted. "Back to Dottie. She's dead? How? When?"

"Well, let me tell you." Aunt Butty slathered on strawberry preserves and took a bite. "Delicious. Now, where was I? Oh, yes. She was found in Hyde Park this morning laying stone cold dead in the middle of a footpath, a hatpin straight through her heart."

I stared at her, mouth hanging open, feeling... I don't know what. Frozen, perhaps? "How do you know?"

"Louise was walking Peaches early this morning. Said the place was crawling with bobbies."

"Louise. Of course," I murmured.

Louise Pennyfather was Aunt Butty's dearest friend. She lived very close to Hyde Park and often walked her dog there.

"Girl was murdered sometime last night or early this morning. Don't know what she was doing in the park alone, but heavens, such a shock. I mean, to stab a person. With a hat pin! Oh, and it was heart-shaped."

"What was?"

"The hatpin," she said around a mouthful of toast. "Or rather, the head of the hatpin."

"How... odd." It was all I could manage. I suddenly wished for something much stronger than coffee. Was it too early to add whiskey? "I wonder who killed her?"

"According to the police, it was her husband."

"*What?*" It came out more like a shriek.

Aunt Butty winced. "Yes. The police arrested him this morning. For murder."

The local police station loomed gray and gloomy against the winter sky. An ancient fortress of terror and doom. I laughed at my own fanciful notion. It was a public building like any other. Despite the gargoyle that leered at me from a drain spout.

Aunt Butty stomped up the stairs behind me, brolly clutched in one hand. It wasn't raining at the moment, but the skies could open up at any time and she was not one to be caught out. Not to mention she could wield the thing better than any swordsman.

The doors were in need of oiling and the foyer stank of wet wool and dirty socks. I wrinkled my nose against the smell, but marched to the front desk, undeterred.

The desk sergeant gave me a startled—and somewhat horrified—look. Apparently, he remembered me from my previous visit, though it had been a few months. "Lady, er, Rample, was it?"

"Yes, Sergeant." I rapped my knuckles against the desk dramatically. "I've come to see Hale Davis."

He rubbed his bald head in confusion. "Who?"

I sighed heavily. "He was brought in for murder. Falsely accused, I might add."

"Oh." The confusion cleared. "That's DCI North's collar."

"As in, Detective Inspector North?" I asked. I'd had a run-in with North during the jazz club finagle.

"Detective *Chief* Inspector North," the sergeant corrected me. "He got a promotion and he's very particular about that."

"As he should be. Well, can I see him?"

"He's a bit busy, my lady." The sergeant fidgeted.

I snorted. "Nonsense. He won't be too busy to see me. Tell him he's got a visitor."

The sergeant looked a little pale, but he obligingly disappeared through a swinging door. I knew from past experience the door led to the work area which North had referred to as the bullpen. I tapped my foot against the marble floor as I waited.

Aunt Butty, on the other hand, had taken a seat in one of the uncomfortable-looking straight-backed chairs lining the wall. She calmly propped reading glasses on the end of her nose, then pulled out knitting needles and a skein of yellow yarn and began knitting away, the needles making little clacking noises.

I stared at her for a moment. "Since when did you take up knitting?"

"My grandmother taught me when I was a girl. She always said idle hands are the devil's work. Naturally, I quit the minute I left home, rather enjoying the devil's work as I do, but recently I realized it gives me something to do when I'm bored. Plus, handmade things make excellent gifts, don't you think?" She held up what I could only guess was an attempt at a scarf, but not only was the color hideous, the thing was misshapen, lumpy, and looked like it might unravel should one look at it cross-eyed.

"Er, yes, well, who is it for?" Dreading her answer.

"I thought Chaz. His birthday is soon, isn't it?"

"Oh, yes. Next month. I'm sure he'll be thrilled."

Charles "Chaz" Raynott would most definitely *not* be thrilled. He was my best friend and sometime partner in crime, and the very epitome of gentleman's fashion. He would be as horrified by the yellow blob as I was. And since we spent a great deal of time together, he'd have to wear it frequently or risk offending Aunt Butty, which he would never do.

Aunt Butty gave me the eye, but remained silent, her needles clicking away. DCI North was taking an inordinately long time. I began to pace, too keyed up to be still.

It felt an age, though had probably been only ten minutes, before the sergeant returned, North trailing along behind him. The detective looked much the same. He was of medium height, medium build, medium looks, and medium coloring. Absolutely forgettable except for his eyes which were hard, cold, and saw far too much.

He gave me a squinty-eyed look. "Lady Rample. What the devil are you doing here?" He did not sound pleased.

"I've come about the Dottie Davis murder."

He lifted a brow. "Oh, yes? You've got information?"

"No. I am here to tell you Hale Davis is innocent."

North snorted. "Hardly. The husband done it. Easy as."

I gritted my teeth. "He didn't. He's not the type to go around murdering people."

"Everybody's the type. First thing you learn in this business."

I was about to blow a gasket when Aunt Butty set aside her knitting. "Detective Chief Inspector North."

He turned to stare at her and she gave him a little finger wave. I swear he blushed. "Er, Aunt, I mean, Lady Butty."

She tittered like a school girl. "Close enough. Now, I understand you believe Mr. Davis murdered his wife. What is your evidence?"

"I'm sorry, but I can't tell you that." North actually looked terrified. Which meant he was smarter than I'd given him credit for.

"Very well." She stared at him over her reading glasses like he was a naughty school boy. "But surely bail has been set?"

"No, my lady. He's a foreigner." As if that explained everything.

She hmphed and North blanched. She tapped her chin with one finger and he actually backed away a step before catching himself.

"Perhaps we can see him?" she suggested. "Or at the very least, allow Ophelia to see him."

"Sorry, can't do that. No visitors except his solicitor." He fidgeted.

"But he does have one?" I asked.

He tugged his collar. "Not at the moment," he admitted.

Aunt Butty stood up, sending both North and the sergeant scrambling. She stuffed her knitting into her enormous green bag which matched her ghastly hat. "Well, we shall see about that. Come, Ophelia." And she sailed out the door like the very buxom prow of a sailing ship.

There was nothing I could do but follow her out, leaving the two policemen staring in our wake. Just before the door swung shut behind me, I heard North mutter, "Well, that was a close one."

One day, I wanted to be just like Aunt Butty.

Chapter 3

Aunt Butty marched straight to my motorcar and climbed in without saying a word. Meanwhile I headed for the red phone box outside the station and put in a call to Varant, whose butler answered on the third ring.

"His lordship is not available," he said, rather huffily, I thought. Then he hung up before I could ask to leave a message. I'm fairly certain the man did not approve of me.

"Varant isn't at home, so that's out," I said as I got behind the wheel and gave Aunt Butty a long, hard stare. "What are you up to?"

She didn't answer but stared straight ahead. "Drive to Louise's."

Since she had that look that said I would get nothing more out of her, I started the car and pulled out into traffic. A horn blared behind me. I ignored it.

"I don't know what Louise Pennyfather is supposed to do about it." Louise was a bit of a character and frankly, a terrible influence on my aunt. Or perhaps it was the other way 'round. Either way, they managed to get up to all sorts of shenanigans when in each other's company.

"Louise may not be able to do much, but her husband can," Aunt Butty said meaningfully.

She was no doubt correct. Mr. Pennyfather did something mysterious which involved a lot of travel for the government. I often suspected he worked with Varant who also did something mysterious for the government—sans travel, typically—though neither gentleman would confirm or deny. It was most frustrating.

I barreled through the narrow streets of London, occasionally blasting my horn at those who annoyed me, as one does. Aunt Butty hung on to her hat with one hand and her handbag with the other, quietly muttering under her breath. I do not think her words were repeatable in company.

Turning down a street lined with elegant Georgian houses, I nearly barreled over a workman crossing the street. He gave me the finger. I gave him one back. And we each went cheerfully on our way.

At last I pulled up to Louise's house and Aunt Butty let out a sigh of relief. "I do wonder who taught you to drive."

"Felix, of course." Felix being my late husband. He'd taught me the basics, being of the mind that women should know how to take care of themselves, up to and including driving. I took it from there.

The Pennyfathers lived in a Georgian townhouse similar to mine across the street from a small, private park. Their door and shutters were painted forest green, while the walls were cream to match the rest of the houses which marched up and down the street like identical soldiers.

We hadn't had time to rap on the door when it swung open revealing Louise in a wildly patterned muumuu clutching a small dog to her chest. It yapped excitedly.

"Hush, Peaches," Louise ordered the dog in stentorian tones before issuing another order to the young maid hovering in the hall behind her. "Take their coats, Gladys. There's a girl. Come. There's tea in my own personal drawing room."

"How'd you know we were coming, darling?" I asked, knowing Aunt Butty hadn't rung her.

Louise turned her long, narrow face toward me. She'd the unfortunate overbite of much of the aristocracy which gave her a rather horse-like appearance. She was a lovely woman, but handsome she was not.

"It was in the cards, dear. I read them this morning. It was very clear." And as if that settled things, she strode into the drawing room.

Cards? I mouthed to Aunt Butty who only shrugged helplessly.

Louise's private sitting room was a little snug at the back of the house. A merry fire burned in the grate. Next to it sat a cozy armchair covered in mauve velvet with a matching footstool. Within easy reach was a round games table over which was draped an exotic floral shawl edged in black fringe. Instead of holding a game, tarot cards were spread out across it in a cross pattern. I hadn't taken Louise for the superstitious type.

"Sit, sit." She waved at the mauve velvet settee across from the grate, and Aunt Butty and I sat obediently. A rosewood coffee table was laden with a silver tea service and trays loaded with tea sandwiches, biscuits, and an entire Victoria sponge on a crystal cake stand. Maybe the cards really had told her we were coming.

"Let me guess," Louise said as she poured tea. "You've come about that paramour of yours."

"Former," I clarified. "Don't tell me the cards gave that away, too."

She snorted inelegantly. "Hardly, dear. I read the paper."

"Oh." I snagged a spice biscuit and bit into it. It had just a touch too much cinnamon, but since someone had been heavy handed with the sugar, I wasn't going to complain.

"Now tell me. What's happening with the investigation?"

It was no surprise whatsoever that Louise thought we were investigating something.

"Nothing," I assured her. "We tried to get in to see Hale, but that dratted North won't let me anywhere near him. Nor will they let him out on bail."

"Detective Chief Inspector North," Aunt Butty clarified, taking the massive slice of cake Louise offered her. "Right full of himself, that one."

"How do you want me to help?" Louise asked, leaning back in her chair and taking a sip of tea. Peaches had taken up residence in front of the grate and was snoring softly.

"We were hoping you might have a word with Mr. Pennyfather," Aunt Butty said, referring to Louise's husband. "Perhaps he has some pull?"

She mulled it over. "While I doubt he can get anyone out of jail, I'm certain he can get you in to see him. Gladys!" She raised her voice in a bellow.

The girl appeared, looking rather terrified. "Yes, madame?"

"Bring me the 'phone immediately," Louise said imperiously.

Gladys looked like she might hyperventilate. "The cord won't reach, madame."

"Good lord, must I do everything myself?" Without waiting for an answer, Louise rose from her seat and strode from the room. Within moments, her strident voice floated back.

"I don't care if he's meeting with the Prime Minister himself. Get my husband on the line this instant, or I shall have you dismissed!"

Apparently, the fear of Louise Pennyfather was greater than the fear of the PM, for within seconds it was clear her husband had come on the line, although her tone didn't change. "There you are. Something must be done... There's been a murder... No, no one we know... Ophelia is involved... Ophelia, Lady Rample, dear. You've met on numerous occasions... Butty's niece... Yes, that's the one... No, of course she didn't murder anyone. It was her lover."

I winced both at the use of the term and at the implied accusation against Hale's innocence. Aunt Butty helped herself to another rather large slice of cake.

"No, dearest, I realize you can't get him out of jail... Of course not. Wouldn't dream of it... I simply want you to get Ophelia in to see him... Really? Excellent... Yes, I will see you tonight. Cook is serving roast duck."

Louise's heels did not click across the foyer, but rather clomped forcefully. She was one of those people you expected would live in the country and ride to the hounds, but she much preferred the city and detested horses. An oddity among English society.

"It's done," she announced as she reentered the room and took her seat. "He'll arrange for you to visit in the morning."

"Thank you, darling." The thought of Hale languishing another night in a jail cell didn't sit right with me, but there wasn't much that could be done. So I snagged a second biscuit.

Over more tea, biscuits, and cake, we discussed the ghastly details of Dottie Davis's death, Hale Davis's arrest, and what it all could mean. At some point Louise brought out the sherry.

"I think we must first figure out who had a motive to kill Dottie Davis," my aunt said, holding out her empty sherry glass for a refill.

"That's easily done," Louise said, obliging. "They always say to look at the husband."

"Which is exactly where they did look, but I know Hale is innocent," I said.

"Very well, let's say that he is," Louise said easily, refilling her own glass, "who is next?"

"Ophelia." Aunt Butty nodded in my direction.

"Don't be daft." I shot her a glare and snagged another biscuit.

"Think about it. You had a very close, personal relationship with her husband," Aunt Butty said.

"They weren't married at the time," I pointed out.

"Even better," Louise said. "You have an excellent motive. Jealousy." She picked up the tarot cards and shuffled them before laying one on the table. "Yes, you see. The Moon." She tapped the card with her fingernail. "It represents jealousy."

I wondered if she was stacking the deck. "Nonsense. I'm not jealous of Dottie. I've no wish to be married again. Men are very lovely until you marry them. Then they become tiresome and tell you what to do with your own money." Although, of course, I was jealous of the fact that Dottie got to be with Hale and I didn't, I supposed.

"What's the motive for the murder?" Aunt Butty asked.

Louise shuffled the deck and laid down another card. She looked up, face a mask. "Seven of Swords."

"What does that mean?" I asked.

Her expression was dark. "Revenge."

I am not typically an early riser, but the next morning found me at the front desk of the police station at precisely nine in the morning. Despite a fairly late evening with Aunt Butty, I was eager to see Hale. And not just to ask him about the murder, though that was certainly part of it.

If Louise's cards were to be believed—and I wasn't entirely sure they were—the motive for Dottie's murder was revenge. Aunt Butty and I had gone over the matter at some length and had come to the conclusion that the one person who might want revenge was Hale himself. Which I didn't believe for a moment. But there it was. Hard to argue with facts, especially since North was already headed in that very obvious direction.

North himself met me and very reluctantly led me through the bullpen to the cells. "This is against my better judgement," he said rather waspishly.

"I thought your job was to collect evidence, not judge," I said with a pointed look.

He glared at me from under his bushy brows. I was fairly certain he muttered something rude, but his mustache was large enough to hide the movement of his lips.

"Maybe you should mind your own potatoes," North muttered.

I ignored him, as I often did. I knew it annoyed him. He showed me to the very last cell where Hale sat, elbows on knees, looking morose. He glanced up as North rattled a key in the lock.

"You got a visitor." He waved me in then locked the cell behind me, which caused a frisson of unease. "I'll be down the hall. Yell when you're ready." And he strode off.

Hale slowly rose. "Ophelia. What are you doing here?"

"Heard you got yourself in a spot of bother, darling."

"I didn't do it."

"I know."

He was across the cell in two steps and took me in his arms, burying his face against my neck. He inhaled deeply, then let me go so suddenly I staggered a bit.

"I'm sorry." He shoved his hands in his pockets. "I shouldn't have done that."

I wanted to tell him it was perfectly fine. That it was what I wanted. That I wanted more. But there was so much between us that was in need of sorting, and his wife was, well, dead. Murdered.

"How are you?" I asked instead.

He shrugged. "Well as can be expected, I guess. I'm a bit shocked. Everything..." He shook his head. "I don't know what's going on."

I sat down on the cot and waited for him to join me. When he did, I said, "That's what I'm here about. What happened with Dottie?" Her name left a nasty taste in my mouth.

"The police say someone murdered her."

"Please, darling. What happened after you left France." *Left me.*

He scrubbed his hands over his face. "She told me she was pregnant with my child, so we got married the day after I returned to London. And then she had a miscarriage."

"I'm so sorry, Hale." How devastating that must have been for him. Except—

"Don't be," he said dryly. "Turns out she was never pregnant at all. She just thought if she married me, she'd get a free ride to America." He snorted. "Not anytime soon. I got no plans to go back. I'm booked for the next six months at The Lion Club. Or at least, I was. Hopefully they won't sack me."

"She lied to you?" The thought was horrifying. I knew women did it, but I thought it was ridiculous. And frankly, it indicated a woman of no character or morals. "How did you find out?"

"A friend of hers. Kitty Leonard. She told me the truth."

"Interesting. I wonder why this Kitty was so forthcoming?"

"No idea," he admitted. "But I was angry when I found out. I left Dottie. Went and stayed with one of my new bandmates. Been staying there since."

My first thought was, "Why didn't he call me?" I stuffed that down for later examination. Right now we had bigger fish to fry. No wonder the police thought him guilty. The woman had lied to him, tricked him into marriage, and then when he found out he'd left her.

"What about the night she was killed? Don't you have an alibi?"

"Sure. But the police won't listen."

I stiffened my spine. "Well, they'll have to listen to me. Tell me, and I'll check it out. Prove to them you're telling the truth."

"You'd do that for me?"

"Of course I would. I still—" *Love you. Care about you.* "I still believe in justice."

"I was at a pub in Chinatown."

"There are pubs in Chinatown?" I asked, surprised. It was not somewhere ladies generally went. Not that ladies generally visited pubs, either.

"There are pubs everywhere."

"Which pub was it?"

"I think it was called the Golden Lilac."

I lifted a brow. "What sort of pub name is that?"

"Well, maybe it was the Golden Flower. I don't remember."

"Very well." I stood from the cot and adjusted the cuffs of my gloves. "Leave it with me. I'll have you out of here in no time at all."

He stood, and I half expected him to kiss me. But he didn't. He shook my hand like a bloody gentleman. "Thank you, Ophelia. I owe you one."

"You're gonna owe me more than one, doll face." Then I sashayed from the cell. Let him see what he'd been missing.

Chapter 4

After I left the police station, I motored over to the block of flats near St. James's park that Chaz called home. The building was only about ten years old and a top-notch example of Art Deco architecture. The walls were smooth, white concrete and curved extravagantly inward at the front. The doors were framed in brass, and a grated elevator squeaked and rattled its way from the ground floor to the sixth floor with excruciating slowness. I took the stairs.

I pounded on the door to flat 6A, somewhat out of breath. There was a pause, then Chaz himself opened the door in his shirtsleeves with smears of shaving cream still on his face. "Ophelia, old thing, whatever are you doing here?"

We exchanged air kisses, and then I sallied into his sitting room. He had a nice view of the park, a lovely tile grate, and enough room for a substantially sized divan, though he'd opted for club chairs instead.

"Darling, I need your help."

"Of course you do, love. Let me just finish up, and I'll be with you. You know where the drinks cupboard is." And he disappeared down the hall.

I helped myself to whiskey neat since he didn't have any ice or ginger ale. Sinking into one of his club chairs, I toasted myself by the fire, enjoying the music wafting from his radio at the back of the flat. I was nearly done with my drink by the time he rejoined me, properly shaved and attired.

"What sort of help do you need?" He asked, refreshing my drink before pouring himself one. "Let me guess. You need to break into the Tower of London and save Hale from the hangman's noose."

"Don't be overly dramatic," I said tartly, though I suddenly realized that if I couldn't prove Hale's alibi, the hangman might become an actuality. I shivered unpleasantly.

"Hale has an alibi. He was at a pub in Chinatown. The Golden Flower or something like that. If we can find someone who saw him there, North will be forced to let him go."

"And you want me to come with you to protect your honor."

"Something like that." While women weren't exactly banned from pubs, or at least not all pubs, they were generally shunned to the far corners. And certainly proper ladies weren't seen in pubs—perish the thought. Not that I gave two figs for what proper ladies did or did not do, but in this particular case, having a man along would certainly help me get answers. Beside which, Chinatown wasn't exactly a safe place for a lady alone after dark. I didn't imagine it was much better in daylight.

"Very well. I shall squire you about." He held out his arm. "Shall we?"

I laughed at his nonsense. "Finish your drink first."

He tossed it back. "No time like the present. Hurry it up, love. Time's a-wasting."

I sighed and drained my class. "Have you somewhere more important to be?"

"Not until tonight." He waggled his eyebrows. "But do you really want your lover wasting away in prison?"

"Don't call him that."

"What? Your lover?" He drew out the last word.

I smacked him. "Don't be a tease. Now help me on with my coat, and let's get going."

Once properly attired for the weather, I drove us across to Chinatown which was basically across the street from the theaters of the West End. Brick buildings packed tight together boasted vibrantly colored signs in Chinese. Fortunately for our purposes, most were translated to English, or at the very least had clear indicators of the type of business inside.

We walked the streets, looking for any sign of a Golden something. There were plenty to choose from: The Golden Dragon, The Golden Star, the Golden Noodle.

"Look. The Golden Lotus." Chaz pointed at a rather dodgy looking building, its bricks black with soot. It looked like no one had cleaned it since the dawn of the Industrial Revolution. "Do you suppose that's it?"

"Looks like. A lotus is a flower, or so I hear." I eyed the building warily.

"Doesn't look like the sort of place they let in women," Chaz said.

I snorted. "Such misogyny. Come along, darling." I strode straight for the door and yanked it open. Smoke billowed out, and I choked, tearing up against the stink. Most of it was tobacco, but there was something sweeter underneath. "Is that—?"

"Opium," Chaz said grimly.

"Oh, dear," I murmured. Chaz once had a problem with opium. "You probably shouldn't go in there."

He straightened his shoulders. "We're doing this for Hale. I'll be fine." But his face was a little pale and there were beads of sweat at his hairline. I didn't like it one bit, but it was his choice.

"Right behind you."

As we walked into the dimly lit room, all conversation stopped, and all eyes turned to stare at us. The barman pointed a thick finger at me and said, "She ain't wanted."

"Maybe you better wait outside, Ophelia," Chaz said softly.

"But—"

"I'm more likely to get the information we need from these gentlemen without you here."

I glanced around at all those cold, hard eyes and realized he was right. I didn't like it though. "Fine. I'll be just outside. If anyone causes you a problem, there will be problems for him." And I gave them all a hard stare before turning about and marching for the door.

The minute I was outside, I drew a deep breath of fresh air—as fresh as it gets in London anyway—relieved to be out of there. What a horrid place! I was shocked that Hale would frequent such an establishment. But then, I really didn't know what had been going on in his life over the last couple of months.

The scent of sweet buns tickled my nose and my stomach rumbled, reminding me that tea at Louise's had been hours ago. I figured it would take Chaz some time to get the information, and the area looked safe enough, so I wandered over to the building from which emanated the delicious aromas.

The brick facade was decorated with a gold and red sign in Chinese. I'd no idea what it meant, but the goods in the window spoke for themselves. I stepped into the steamy interior and everyone turned to stare at me. This was becoming an uncomfortable routine.

I was the only Westerner in the place. Everyone else was Chinese and wore Chinese-style clothing. I stood out like a sore thumb. Instead of creeping out, I lifted my head and marched straight to the counter.

"I'd like one of those, please." I pointed randomly to one of the buns sitting in neat stacks in wicker baskets along the front of the shop.

The tiny little woman behind the counter bowed and then used a set of tongs to extract a bun which she dropped into a paper bag. Then she rattled out a few words which I didn't at all understand.

"Oh, dear. Let me see what I've got." I pulled out my coin purse and began to show her various coins. She just stared at me.

"It's just a farthing, miss," a voice from behind me spoke.

I turned to see a very pretty young Chinese girl dressed in a simple blue cotton dress with a high mandarin collar. "My grandmother doesn't speak English."

"As I don't speak your language, I'm afraid," I said apologetically. I selected a bronze coin and handed it to the grandmother who bowed again. "Please tell her thank you."

The girl rattled off a few words which resulted in more bowing. I found myself bowing back and hoped neither of them took offence. They didn't seem to. Instead the girl asked, "Have you had our buns before?"

"I haven't, but their delightful smell lured me over."

She grinned. "I hope you enjoy them then."

"Oh, I'm sure I shall." I eyed her closely. She was young, spoke flawless English, obviously worked here. Long hours no doubt. Perhaps she had seen Hale. "I was wondering... perhaps you might help me. My name is Ophelia."

"Mai Lin."

"Oh, what a lovely name. Well, Mai Lin, a friend of mine was down here the other night. Perhaps you saw him?" I described Hale. "I believe he spent some time in the Golden Lotus."

Mai Lin shook her head. "Sorry, not me." She spoke a few words to her grandmother. I expected a negative answer, but after a little back and forth, Mai said, "Yes. Grandmother saw him."

My jaw nearly dropped. "She did? When? Where?"

More back and forth with a great deal of wild gesturing from the grandmother.

"She says it was two nights ago. Very late. She was shutting up shop when she saw Mr. Ling throw this man out of the Golden Lotus. He was quite drunk and refused to leave."

"Does she know what time this was?" My heart beat excitedly.

"She says it was around ten o'clock. That's when she went home that night."

"Did she see where he went?" I asked. According to North, Dottie had been killed sometime between ten and midnight, which didn't really help Hale's case.

Mai Lin pointed to a park bench at the curb. "He laid down there and went to sleep. She doesn't know how long he was there since she went straight home."

I gave them both a smile and thanked them profusely before returning to my waiting spot outside the Golden Lotus. As I waited, I nibbled on the bun. It was lovely, light and sweet, with a creamy, exotic filling. I recognized it as coconut. Something I'd only had a few times but was inordinately fond of. I would have to remember to come back to this bakery.

I had just finished my bun when Chaz came out. I told him about my trip to the bakery and gave him a quick run-down on what the old lady had told me. "What did you find out?"

"The barman says he threw Hale out at ten for being too deep in his cups."

"Wholly unlike Hale," I said. "But it does put us in a bit of a bind. It still doesn't give him an alibi."

"True, but one of the other patrons assured me that if anyone saw him, it was Win."

"Win? What sort of a name is Win?"

Chaz shrugged. "No idea, but he has a little bookshop over on Coventry. We can walk over. It's not far."

"Very well," I said, not at all thrilled about the idea. My idea of exercise is lifting a cocktail glass.

Coventry Street was a couple of blocks down, past the China Gate which loomed above, it's tiered roof lines of terra cotta tiles and brightly colored frontage gleaming in the late afternoon sun. Win's bookshop was right on the corner in the ground floor of an old Victorian building, the bricks of which were stained nearly black—like those at the Golden

Lotus—from decades of London fog. There was no sign, only simple letters on the door that read *Win's Books*.

"Creative," I muttered dryly.

"Don't be a drip," Chaz muttered back. "We need his help, remember?"

I sighed. "Very well, darling, but I can't help it if people are boring."

Inside, the shop smelled strongly of tinned sardines, cigarettes—which I detest—and old books. There was also a rather plump black cat sitting on the counter. It glared at me through slitted green eyes. I stared back, and I swear it smirked at me.

Books of all sizes and shapes were stacked about the shop in tottering piles. A few rickety shelves, crammed to overflowing, lined the walls while a large table, stacked nearly to the ceiling, took up the center of the room. Even the way to the counter was half blocked by books.

There was no one in the shop. No buyers or browsers. No one even stuck their head in. And there was no sign of the proprietor, Win.

Chaz cleared his throat and shouted out, "Hello? Anyone in? We're here for Win." He grimaced at the inadvertent rhyme even as I snickered.

From behind the counter rose first an orange and black Chinese silk cap with orange tassels hanging from its crown. That was followed by a round face with small, dark eyes and an enormous, drooping mustache with a pipe poking from beneath it. He was not Chinese, as I had assumed, but very obviously English.

He pulled the pipe from his lips. "'ullo. Looking for a book, are we? Come to the right place."

Had he been napping back there? I coughed as a cloud of smoke billowed my way.

Since I was having trouble speaking for once in my life, Chaz took over, explaining our conundrum. "Chap down at the Golden Lotus said maybe you could help."

Win tugged at his mustache. "Black fellow, you say? American? Oh, aye. I remember 'im quite well. Got himself absolutely soused. Over a woman, I reckon. Always a woman. Sorry, ma'am."

I waved him off, thinking he likely wasn't entirely wrong, and stepped back a few paces to give myself breathing room. I pretended to peruse what appeared to be the travel section. There was a book about Paris. I flipped through a few pages, then set it down quickly when I realized it was more about Parisian women than Paris itself. And they all seemed to be lacking in clothing.

"So, you did see him, then?" Chaz's voice caught my attention.

"Sure and certain," Win said around his pipe. "Found 'im passed out on the bench, didn't I?"

"What time was that?" Chaz asked.

Win stared up at the ceiling as if it might give him inspiration. "Oh, 'bout half ten."

Thirty minutes. Thirty minutes to walk to Hyde Park, murder Dottie, and get back to the bench for Win to find him. Could it be done?

I calculated quickly in my mind. Very unlikely. Both the barman and Win claimed Hale was drunk out of his mind. And while he might be able to fool Win, I doubted he'd be able to fool an experienced barman. Leaving that aside, it would take more than thirty minutes to walk from the Golden Lotus to Hyde Park. Even if he'd been able to catch a cab, it would still have been at least fifteen minutes each way, not to mention having to walk to the center of the park to kill Dottie. No, there was simply no way that he could have done it in that time frame. If that's the time she died.

"Did you see him after that?" I asked.

Win squinted at me. "Well, sure 'nough I did. It was cold, you see. Couldn't leave the poor man sitting there to freeze to death. Wouldn't be Christian. So, I roused 'im and got 'im to the shop, you see. Hot tea does the trick."

I was feeling a little faint. "What time did he leave the shop?"

"He didn't. Not til morning. He slept on my cot right here."

We both peered over the counter to find that there was indeed a cot back there.

"Where'd you sleep?" Chaz asked.

"Upstairs, o'course. Got a nice little flat above the shop."

"How do you know he didn't sneak out sometime during the night, then come back in later?"

"Couldn't," Win said firmly. "Door's locked after closing. No way out 'less you've got a key, and he ain't got one. I let him out at six the next morning."

Chaz and I exchanged glances. We'd done it. We'd proved Hale's alibi. Now we just had to convince North.

Chapter 5

It took some doing to convince Win to leave his shop and come to the police station with us, but we finally managed. I even let him smoke in my car, which I wasn't thrilled about, but needs must.

We got a lot of stares while we waited for North. I don't suppose it's every day one sees an Englishman in a Chinese outfit smoking a pipe while sitting with two of the aristocracy in the waiting area of a police station. For Win's part, he seemed entirely unperturbed by the stares.

"Did you used to live in China?" I asked by way of conversation.

"Nope."

I glanced at his outfit, basically a pair of thick, silk pajamas. "I see." I didn't.

Win chuckled. "Doubt it. These things are damned—er, 'scuse me ma'am—darned comfortable. Everyone will be wearing them one day."

I doubted that, although I thought they'd make a rather nice pair of beach pajamas. Or perhaps some lovely loungewear. They did look comfortable. I made a mental note to make another trip to Chinatown. And not just for those delicious buns.

At last North appeared, looking put out by our very presence. He grew more morose by the minute once he learned that not only did Hale have an alibi, but that we could prove it. And although Win was a little eccentric, he was a proper, tax-paying citizen of Britain, and there was nothing North could do to deny his claim that he had played host to a drunken Hale.

"I guess we'll have to let him go," he finally admitted.

"Don't look so disappointed," I snapped. "Maybe if you'd done your job properly, you wouldn't be in this state of embarrassment."

I realized, as North's eyes narrowed, that perhaps I'd pushed the detective a bit too far this time. If I wasn't careful, he'd be pointing the finger at me just to be contrary. I flinched as he scraped back his chair and stalked toward me.

"Ophelia, Lady Rample," he intoned. "I am placing you under arrest."

"Oh, I say!" Chaz cried. "That's not on, my good man."

"Why?" I sneered. "Because I did your job?"

"No," he gritted. "Because you murdered Dottie Davis."

I should have known better than to get North in a lather. To say I wasn't best pleased with my new accommodations is perhaps the understatement of the century. Upon placing me under arrest, he had immediately marched me back to processing. After being photographed and fingerprinted, he stuffed me in a cell not unlike the one where I'd visited Hale. At least he'd let me keep my own clothes, and I hadn't been forced into one of those striped overalls one always sees prisoners wearing in films.

Naturally, he had his reasons for arresting me. I'd been Hale's lover. Dottie had stolen him from me. I'd suffered a blind, jealous rage. We'd had a row at The Lion Club. And so forth.

It was all ridiculous nonsense, of course. What it really boiled down to was that North didn't much like me ever since I'd solved the crime he should have done. And I didn't have an alibi. Not a good one anyway.

While Dottie Hale had been getting herself murdered, I was at home, asleep. Well, I assumed I was asleep. After Varant had dropped me off, I'd enjoyed a nightcap or two before going to bed to read. According to North, there'd been plenty of time between my arriving at home and Dottie's death for me to slip out and do the deed. Unfortunately, Maddie had been sound asleep and hadn't even heard me come in. Wonderful. The one time I needed my nosey maid, she failed me.

I slumped on the rather uncomfortable cot and stared morosely at the wall. There was a stain that looked just like Italy. Italy. Now there was a place I should visit. If they didn't hang me for murder first.

"Get ahold of yourself, Ophelia," I said aloud. "You are made of sterner stuff than this. You will find a way out of this mess."

And yet, I'd no idea how. Locked up in here, I couldn't do any investigating. I hadn't even seen Hale, although North had assured me they'd let him go.

Time ticked slowly by, the shadows lengthening. I was glad for my winter coat as it was rather chilly inside the cell. Really, you'd think they could heat it better or at least give a person a decent blanket. I eyed the one in my cell askance. It looked very like it might have an infestation.

Since I'd nothing better to do, I decided to go over the facts as I knew them.

Fact one: Dottie had lied to Hale about having his child and had tricked him into marriage. Which gave him a clear motive. Although he had an alibi and was therefore innocent. Did it give anyone else a motive?

Fact two: She'd picked a very public fight with me mere hours before her death. Well, not so much a fight as a lot of fist waving and posturing. Why? She'd never met me before. How did she know who I was? Or that I was there that night? And why confront me so publicly? She'd only embarrassed herself.

Fact three: She'd visited Hyde Park in the middle of the night. Why? Ladies, as a general rule, did not visit parks alone at night. Not that she'd been a lady, but still. Had she gone there with someone? Or perhaps to meet someone?

Fact four: Somewhere between ten at night and two in the morning, someone had stabbed Dottie Davis through the heart with a heart-shaped hat pin. Hat pins were generally the purview of women. Had her murder been a spur-of-the-moment thing and the killer used what was to hand? Then the killer was almost certainly a woman. Or had the killer brought the pin for the specific purpose of ending Dottie's life? If that was the case, it would mean the killer could be either a man or a woman.

Fact five: Hale Davis was innocent. Of that I was sure. He not only had an alibi, thanks to Win, but I couldn't believe him capable of a cold-blooded killing like that. Obviously, I was also innocent. Which left... who?

The problem was I knew nothing about Dottie. I'd never met her before that night at the Lion Club. I hadn't even known her pregnancy was fake or her marriage was on the skids until that night. In fact, I hadn't even known her name. Which meant I had no idea what she was like, who her friends were, or if she might have angered someone enough to kill her, either out of spontaneous rage or cold planning. Was she the type to incite violence in others?

Based on my brief encounter with her, I'd have to say yes. She'd been coarse and common, but I didn't hold that against her. That was a matter of birth and circumstance. But there'd been something in her expression. Something that told me she'd reveled in causing that scene. In making the people around her uncomfortable. If she was happy to do that to a complete stranger—me—then what might she do to someone she actually knew and on whom she might have some delicious dirt?

The problem was I didn't know who Dottie was close to, other than Hale and, apparently, some women called Kitty Leonard. I had no idea where she lived, who her friends were, or how she spent her time. Hale might know those things, but so far, he was a no-show. I would have been more upset about it, but knowing North, he probably wasn't letting anyone see me. Especially not Hale.

Well, he was going to get an earful from my solicitor come morning. Locking me up without allowing me counsel or a phone call was beyond illegal, and I would make sure he paid for it.

With that jolly thought, I managed to drift off to sleep only to be awoken less than an hour later when the on-duty sergeant ushered a drunk into one of the other cells. She proceeded to sing "The Twelve Days of Christmas" very loudly and off key.

"You do know it's not Christmas," I shouted somewhere between the rings and the calling birds.

There was a pause, a loud belch, and then, "It's always Christmas in my heart."

I held back a laugh. "Well then, carry on."

And she did.

Chapter 6

I must have fallen asleep, because the next thing I knew, the desk sergeant was rattling a key in the lock of my cell. "Good morning, my lady," he said with equal parts cheer and caution. "Come along now. Your bail's been paid."

I sat up, yawning. "I didn't even know it'd been set."

He hesitated. "Well, let's just say things have been sorted and you may go, but you're still under caution and a suspect in the murder of Mrs. Davis." Although, from the expression on his face, he found the whole thing as daft as I did.

"Sure, sure. Don't suppose I could visit the cloakroom first?"

He looked confused.

I sighed. "The toilets."

His expression cleared, although he blushed as he led me down the hall. Once I'd done the necessary and freshened up as best I could in the cloudy mirror above the sink, he guided me through the bullpen to the front. As I passed North's office, I poked my head in. He sat hunched over a newspaper, cup of tea in hand. "I'm not at all impressed with your hospitality."

He clutched his heart. "I am gutted. My life's work is to see you happy."

"Sarcasm does not become you," I snapped, and trotted off to ensure I got in the last word. Petty? Me? Surely you jest.

I found Aunt Butty waiting with Varant in the foyer.

"Chaz called me last night," Aunt Butty said, enfolding me in a hug, crushing me against her ample bosom. "I called Varant immediately. Something must be done about that ghastly North person."

"He was just doing his job," I said, though I wouldn't mind him being taken down a peg. "Thank you,

Varant. I don't know how you managed, but I am grateful." I didn't mention the fact that while he'd somehow worked a miracle for me, he hadn't managed the same with Hale.

He gave an elegant bow. "At my lady's service. Shall I escort the two of you home?"

While he broght us home, I regaled them with my tale of finding Win, freeing Hale, and my night in jail, including the drunken serenade.

"Good heavens!" Aunt Butty said. "It sounds appalling."

"It was an experience," I said. "One I'm very glad to leave in the rearview mirror. Now I just need to find Dottie's killer so North will be forced to unarrest me, or whatever one does."

"I don't think he can unarrest you," Varant said dryly as we pulled out into early morning traffic. "He will have to dismiss the charges, and I will ensure there is a very public apology."

I waved it off. Some might worry that being arrested for murder would tarnish one's reputation, but I knew better. Likely it would only add to my mystique or whatnot. No doubt my invitations to parties and such would double over the next few weeks. At least until the hubbub died down and someone did something equally shocking, like strip off in the House of Lords.

"Do you really think you should be investigating, Ophelia?" my aunt asked. "After all, you are the prime suspect. You don't want to give North any reason to arrest you again."

I snorted. "The man is a ninny. If I leave it to him, I'll end up hanging."

She paled. "Please, Ophelia. My nerves."

I laughed. "You have got nerves of steel, Aunt. Now stop this nonsense. We need to find out all we can about Dottie Davis and her life both before and after she married Hale."

"I will leave the two of you to your investigations," Varant said as he showed us to my front door. "I've got business to attend to."

"Thanks again for riding to my rescue," I said lightly, giving him a peck on the cheek before he strode away. But deep inside, I wondered why he'd come to my rescue so easily, yet ignored my request to help Hale? Could Varant somehow be involved in all this?

It was a ridiculous thought, and I brushed it off before it could take root.

The moment I got home, I left Aunt Butty to her own devices and went straight up to wash off the grime of prison. Once Maddie had drawn my bath and laid out clean clothes, I sent her off to make my aunt a pot of tea and some sandwiches, though I'd no doubt she was already raiding my liquor cabinet despite it being barely gone nine in the morning.

Maddie had added my favorite rose-scented oil to the bath, and I sank into the warm water with a sigh of relief. Now all I needed was a rather substantial glass of whiskey and a magazine, and I'd be set.

Between the warmth and the long night, I'd very nearly dozed off when a banging on the bathroom door startled me awake. "Are you alive in there?"

"Charles Raynott! Don't you dare open that door, or I shall murder you instantly," I shouted, flailing slightly in the water before managing to snag a nearby towel.

There was a chuckle. "Very well, but you'd better hurry it along. The coffee is piping hot and Hale brought croissants. Lord knows where he found them, but they're delicious, and I shall eat them all if you don't move your backside."

Hale was here? "Give me fifteen minutes."

"Five."

"Very well, ten. And there had better be at least two croissants and half a pot of coffee left, or my roses will have a lovely bit of fertilizer."

He laughed. Probably because he knew I didn't have any roses. Well, there was one small rose bush in a pot on the veranda, but it wasn't exactly the sort of place one could hide a body.

Once I heard his footsteps retreating down the hall, I wrapped myself in a robe and scuttled back to my bedroom. I quickly dressed in the peacock blue merino wool Maddie had selected. I slipped on my black patent Cuban-heeled Oxfords with the cute little bows and added a jet necklace and earrings. After checking to make sure the bath hadn't frizzed my hair too badly, I patted my face with a bit of powder, swiped on some pale pink lipstick, and decided that was well enough for a woman who'd just escaped the jailor.

Aunt Butty was entertaining the men in my sitting room, and they all greeted me with a cheer. After snagging a croissant from the tray, I sank onto a chair across from Hale and Chaz. Aunt Butty poured me coffee, and I nearly drained the cup in one go. Exhaustion pulled at me, and the beverage was very welcome.

"Ophelia, I'm glad to see you escaped North's custody none the worse for wear. I'm sorry helping me got you in such a pickle." Hale's dark eyes spoke volumes.

I nodded, unable to speak for a moment. It was such a relief to be free and to have him here. I felt a momentary stab of guilt that the reason he was here was because his wife was dead and somebody had murdered her.

Aunt Butty cleared her throat and clapped her hands. "Now, we must get organized."

"For what?" I asked, nibbling on a croissant slathered in strawberry preserves. Fine, I wasn't nibbling so much as chomping like a starving race horse.

"We must prove your innocence," she declared. "We are all on the case. Isn't that right, boys?"

The two men nodded.

"Of course, we are," Chaz said, helping himself to more coffee. "Can't have our Ophelia swinging for a crime she didn't commit."

I winced. "Thanks for that image."

"We're going to prove it wasn't you, Ophelia," Hale said seriously. "I swear it."

I was relieved that he at least didn't think I'd done it. I hid my momentary lapse of emotion behind a swallow of coffee.

"Where shall we start?" Aunt Butty asked, dusting croissant crumbs off her bosom.

"I think we need to know more about Dottie," I said, avoiding Hale's gaze, uncertain what I would find there. "There had to be someone in her life besides Hale and me who wanted her dead. Not that *we* wanted her dead, but you know what I mean. Someone with motive."

"Could have been random," Chaz mused. "There are killers out that who murder complete strangers."

"Yes," Aunt Butty said. "Remember that dreadful Ripper chap? I mean, obviously it can't be him, but perhaps someone like him."

"Could have been," I admitted. "In which case, it will likely never be solved, but I have a feeling this was very personal. The type of weapon. The closeness of the deed. I think whoever killed her knew her." This time my gaze did slide to Hale's. It was time for him to tell us what he knew. I would have rather done it privately, but I doubted either Aunt Butty or Chaz would give us a chance.

Aunt Butty tapped her reading glasses on the arm of her chair. "Well, Mr. Davis?"

Hale cleared his throat. "To be honest, I don't know that much about Dottie."

Aunt Butty snorted. "You married her."

He rubbed his scalp. "Yes, well, that was a mistake."

"I'll say," muttered Chaz.

"Please, you two," I said to Aunt Butty and Chaz. "Let him tell us what happened."

"As I told Ophelia, I married Dottie immediately upon returning to London. It was only after I found out that not only wasn't she pregnant, but she never had been. I was... angry."

"As well you should be," Aunt Butty said. "How long after you married did you discover her perfidy?"

"Less than a week. I moved out immediately," he continued. "I thought I could get on with my life, but Dottie kept following me around, trying to get me back. I threatened her with divorce. She threatened to destroy my reputation." He shook his head. "I didn't care. I actually met with a lawyer three days before she died. I had grounds and I was going ahead with it."

Relief flooded me. He'd visited a solicitor. He'd been going to end it with her even before all this. But that didn't necessarily mean he'd come back to me.

"I suppose then you didn't learn much about each other during the time you lived together," Aunt Butty said, tapping her chin with her reading glasses.

He shook his head. "Almost nothing. When I wasn't home sleeping, I was either practicing with the band or playing at the club."

"What did she do while you were gone?" Aunt Butty asked.

"No idea," he admitted. "I assumed she was home, but she could have been anywhere, and I'd never know."

"Perhaps we need to backpedal," Chaz suggested, grabbing another croissant from the tray. "Tell us how and where you met her. Her maiden name. Did any of her friends attend the marriage ceremony? Perhaps there's a clue there."

Hale leaned back, hands braced behind his head, stretching his lovely, muscled arms beneath his crisp cotton shirt. I remembered how those arms felt around me, but I shook off the memory trying to focus on what he was saying.

"Her maiden name was Lancaster. We met at one of the clubs where I was playing shortly before I met Ophelia. She was working the coat check, and she'd sneak down to listen to the band play. One thing led to another and... well... I realized my mistake almost immediately. She was clingy and demanding and a little unstable. So I broke it off with her. I met you," he glanced at me, "a week later. I never thought I'd see her again, but somehow she tracked me down in France to tell me she was pregnant."

"She would have been, what, seven months along? How did you not notice she wasn't with child?" Aunt Butty demanded, eyes narrowed.

"She did a very good job of pretending," Hale said dryly. "Made a false stomach from a pillow. Wore maternity clothes. It wasn't like we were..." His cheeks darkened with embarrassment. "The marriage was unconsummated. I couldn't bring myself... it was one thing to marry her so our child would have a father. Being a proper husband, well, I hadn't managed to bring myself around to that yet."

"Alright, so you met her at a club. Did she still work there after your marriage?" Chaz asked, neatly redirecting the conversation.

Clearly relieved, Hale shook his head. "My understanding, according to her friend, was that she was fired from that job shortly after I broke it off with her. I've no idea where or if she's been working since."

"You met one of her friends?" I asked. "What's her name? Do you know how to get hold of her?" Here was the exact clue we were looking for. Someone who knew Dottie. And someone who was obviously not the best of friends since she'd been willing to rat on her. Maybe she could tell us more.

Hale frowned. "I told you about her. Kitty Leonard. I don't have her address, unfortunately."

My heart sank. I'd hoped for something new. Although this Kitty person was obviously someone we needed to speak to.

"Why was she willing to tell you the truth about Dottie if they were supposedly such good friends?" Aunt Butty demanded.

Hale grimaced. "Apparently, Kitty had a boyfriend named Arnie. After I left Dottie, before she tracked me down in France, she apparently stole him from Kitty. Kitty wasn't terribly pleased about that. I guess she wanted payback."

"Crikey," I muttered. "I guess so. What a piece of work." Then I realized that I was talking about his dead wife, and I glanced at him with apology.

He shook his head. "I know. I was stupid."

"No, you were a gentleman. You were trying to do the right thing," I said softly.

Chaz cleared his throat. "Seems to me we've got two people to talk to. Archie and Kitty."

"Like I said, I don't know where Kitty lives, but I do know where we can find Archie."

It was a step in the right direction. And maybe Archie could lead us to the vengeful Kitty. Vengeance, after all, is an excellent motive for murder.

Shéa MacLeod

Chapter 7

Archie Evans owned a garage at the edge of the East End. The building was so dilapidated it was nearly falling down. I was astonished the city hadn't yet condemned it. However, Archie seemed to be doing a rather lucrative trade despite the dodgy locale and drizzly, gray day.

No less than three men in greasy overalls puttered about, heads stuck under the bonnets of various motorcars. Everything from a rusty 1915 Humber, to a nearly new Ace Tourer still wearing a shiny coat of cream paint.

Hale and I made our way carefully across the yard, dodging oil-slicked puddles and ankle-breaking potholes. I was glad he was with me rather than Chaz or Aunt Butty. Both the place and the men looked a little rough, and I'd no doubt Hale could match them for toughness. They'd never respect a toff like Chaz, and Aunt Butty... well, she'd likely have shown up with a cornucopia on her head and been laughed off the lot. Not that she'd have let them run her off, but it's difficult to get information out of people when they're doubled over with laughter.

"Archie Evans?" Hale asked the first man we came to, a weedy gentleman of indeterminate years and watery blue eyes.

He stared at us for a long beat, then pointed across to the next vehicle before turning back to his work without uttering a word.

Archie was hunched over a cherry red '28 Austin Windsor. Gorgeous thing. Felix had considered buying one shortly before his death. I could easily imagine myself racing through the British countryside. He looked up as we approached, a frown crossing his grime-streaked face, no doubt wondering why a lady was picking her way through his garage.

"Archie Evans?" Hale asked, taking the lead.

Clearly Archie approved. He nodded, his unusual gray eyes—bright in his tawny face—taking in our appearance. "What can I do you for?" He didn't bother to offer a hand, which was a relief, seeing as how it was filthy with black grease and would no doubt soil my gloves.

"I understand you knew Dottie Lancaster," Hale said easily.

"Knew," Archie said laconically, wiping his filthy hands on a filthier rag. "What's it to you?"

"I knew her as well."

Archie's expression gave away nothing. "Then you know she's dead."

"I do," Hale admitted.

"Lemme guess," Archie spat on the ground, regardless of the fact there was a lady present. "You're that sap what married her. Told you some sob story I bet."

"Yes, I'm that sap," Hale admitted dryly.

Archie eyed him. "Heard you got done for the killing."

"Alibi."

Archie let out a huff of understanding. "Bound to happen sometime. Woman cheesed off more people than a dozen politicians put together."

I couldn't help but laugh at that.

Archie gave me a look. "And how'd you know her?"

"Let's just say that she and I didn't get along," I said drolly.

"Sounds like Dottie. Never did get along with women."

"But she had a female friend," I pointed out. "Kitty?"

He snorted. "You know what happened between 'em?"

We both shook our heads, wanting to hear his version of the story.

"Well, now, me and Kitty, we go way back, if you get my meaning. Never got married or nothin' but might as well have been."

"But you and Dottie somehow ended up together," Hale said.

Archie swiped the rag across the back of his neck. "'Fraid so. Stupid of me. I knew what she was, but Dottie had been after me for a long time and she was... well, you know how she was. Beautiful and... phew!"

Hale grinned, but I crossed my arms and glared at them. Really, men could be so thick. "So you dumped poor Kitty for Dottie."

"Like I said. Stupid."

At least he was willing to admit it.

"Didn't last long," he continued. "But even though I got myself out after a coupla weeks, Kitty wouldn't take me back. If you ask me, she done it."

"Kitty?" I asked. "You think she killed Dottie?" It totally fit with my theories about vengeance.

"Yup. She was livid over the whole thing. Not that I blame her. Probably killed Dottie out of pure spite. Kitty ain't exactly the forgiving kind."

"You know where we can find her?" Hale asked.

Surprisingly, Archie gave him directions to Kitty's flat in the East End. We thanked him and picked our way back across the lot to my car.

Hale was just opening the door for me when Archie shouted out, "Mind how you go. That woman... she's dangerous."

Hale and I exchanged glances. The ride to Kitty's was very quiet.

Kitty Leonard's flat was above a pie and mash shop. We had to walk through a narrow alley—stinking of rotting rubbish and likely infested with rats—and take a set of rickety steps up to the first floor. I was happier than ever that Hale was with me, even though things were still a little awkward and unsettled between us. We needed to have A Talk, but at the moment, we needed to figure out who killed Dottie.

I rapped on the door which rattled in the frame. Inside, there was a crash, followed by a coarse female voice letting out a string of words that turned the air blue. Finally, the door was yanked open, and a woman stood on the threshold.

She was surprisingly small—no more than five feet tall—with blonde hair done in curlers and skin so pale I wondered if she'd powdered her entire body. Her makeup was garish to the point of being tarty, and she wore a heavy, handknit cardigan over a thin slip. It was not the way a decent sort of person opened the door.

"Whatcha want?" She took a drag on the cigarette that dangled from her red lips and sent a puff of smoke straight into my face.

My eyes watered, but I managed not to cough, keeping a vague smile plastered to my face. We needed information from this woman, and she was clearly not the sort of person who liked competition in either the brains or the beauty department. Something I understood intrinsically. I also understood that while she would pretend not to be impressed by my title, she was just the sort of person who *would* be impressed.

"Ophelia, Lady Rample," I said, holding out my hand.

She stared at it a moment before finally shaking it. She affected being unimpressed, but I could tell she was despite herself. "What'sa toff like you doin' here?"

"Well," I said, pressing my gloved hands together primly, "I am in desperate need of your help."

Her eyes widened a fraction before the mask of indifference fell once again. "Yeah? Whatcha need my help with?" Her gaze flicked to Hale, standing on the step below me. "Don't I know you?"

"Hale Davis." He tipped his hat.

This time, she wasn't able to withhold her surprise. "You're Dottie's husband."

"Was," he corrected. "I'm not sure if you've heard—"

"Yeah, someone done her in. I heard. Can't say I'm surprised." She took another drag on her cigarette, but this time blew smoke away from me.

"The police are useless," I confided.

She snorted. "No surprise there."

"We plan to discover the truth of why Dottie died and who killed her," I said. "And we're hoping you can help us."

Her eyes went to little slits. "Why would I do that?"

"She was your friend, wasn't she?" I asked.

"Until she stole my man," Kitty sneered. "Then she was dead to me." As if realizing how that sounded, her mouth made a little "oh." "Sorry, I mean…"

I waved it off. "Not to worry. *I* understand. But we don't want that nasty detective thinking the wrong thing, do we?" Implying he might be after her next. "Which is why we need your help. After all, you knew her best."

"True. Well, come on in." She stepped back to let us through the door which opened straight into the kitchen.

"Ain't got tea, though." Despite the fact there was a steaming pot sitting on the table just inside the door.

"No worries," I said airily. "We just ate."

We sat at the table in rickety mismatching chairs, ignoring the teapot which smelled of cheap tea and strong tannins and the pack of inexpensive biscuits lying open on the counter. A clothes line strung with undergarments hung over the cooker.

I admit to being rather shocked she would allow us to see her flat in such a state. My mother would have been appalled. Her home was always neat as a pin. Mine was only so because of Maddie and a cleaning woman that came once a week to do for me. Still, judge not and all that. So I settled on my precarious perch and focused on getting what I could out of Kitty.

"How did you and Dottie meet?" I said, pretending my throat didn't itch as Kitty puffed away on her cigarette.

She rubbed the side of her nose. "It was two years ago. We were workin' at this club, see. Nothin' untoward, mind. Just serving drinks, that sort of thing. We got on, see, being of a mind about certain things. So for a while we was flatmates."

"Here?" Hale asked. His voice didn't reflect it, but I got the impression he was surprised.

"Naw. Few streets over in what she called a 'better address.'" Kitty shook her head. "'If you pretend, you'll get there eventually,' she'd always say to me. Stuff and nonsense. No amount of pretending was ever gonna make Dottie more'n she was. Common as muck."

I tried not to laugh. That was like the pot calling the kettle black. "Why did you stop living together?"

"It was the rent. Sky high. Couldn't afford it, and she wouldn't see reason. So I moved out, got me this flat with my boyfriend, Archie. She was madder than anything, but she got over it."

Archie had told the truth then. He had lived here with her. "And you stayed friends? You and Dottie."

"Sure. Until six months ago when she stole Archie right out from under me."

I feigned astonishment and horror. "That's terrible."

"It was. The blighter. But it weren't hardly more'n a week and he were back here, beggin' me to forgive him and take him back."

"And did you?" Hale asked, playing along.

"No sir! Gave him his marching orders, let me tell you."

"I suppose you'd have liked to get a bit of payback," I suggested.

"Well, sure, that'd have been nice, but she got hers in the end, didn't she?" Kitty stubbed out her cigarette and contentedly lit another.

"I suppose she did," I said. "But of course, it wasn't you."

"'Course not. I'm no idiot. I'm not about to hang for the likes of her."

Fair point, although I wasn't sure I bought it. "The police asked about your alibi?"

She snorted. "No police around here. Give it time, and they will be. But I've got a good one. I was right here with my new man. We were getting real cozy like, if you know what I mean." She winked then gave Hale a lascivious look.

I did. Unfortunately. "Oh, you've got a new boyfriend. How lovely for you."

"So you see, no need to go bumping off old Dottie. She was her own worst enemy."

"What do you mean?" asked Hale.

"You know," she said meaningfully. "She pulled her tricks on you. That was Dottie. Cooking up schemes. Getting her hooks in innocent people. Told her that was never gonna get her places, but she wouldn't listen. And look what happened." She didn't seem very broken up about it.

"Do you have any idea who might have wanted to kill Dottie?" I asked.

"Sure. Anyone who ever met her. But if you want to know what I think, I think it was Archie what done her in."

"Why's that?" Hale asked.

"She stole from him, didn't she? Took a wad o' cash right outta his trouser pocket."

Interesting. Archie hadn't mentioned that little fact. I wondered how much Dottie had taken and if it would have made Archie mad enough to kill her. The former boyfriend blamed the former best friend and vice versa. No surprise there.

"Was there somewhere Dottie liked to hang out?" I asked. "Somewhere she might have met someone who..."

"Wanted to kill her?" Kitty blew a cloud of smoke toward the ceiling, those bright red lips pursing just so. Despite her relative youth, tiny lines already formed around her lips. "Well, last I knew, she'd just discovered this new placed called Apollyon. She said a lotta swells hung out there. She was gonna snare herself a new man." She snorted. "She couldn't even keep the one she got." She eyed Hale knowingly.

With nothing else to discover from the woman, we said our goodbyes. I breathed a sigh of relief as we once again inhaled fresh air. It wasn't just the smoky room that had been oppressive. Kitty, with her bad attitude and mean streak, was one of those women I found exhausting.

"Where to now?" I asked as Hale escorted me to the car. "I'm betting this Apollyon place doesn't open for hours yet."

"I won't be able to go with you," he said. "I've got to play tonight."

I understood, but I still felt a slight pang, so I said breezily, "That's alright. I'll bring Chaz along."

"I've got a couple hours before I need to be at the club. Why don't we grab a bite to eat," he suggested. "And talk."

It sounded ominous. But I agreed. We did, indeed, need to talk. I just wasn't sure where or how that talk would go.

Shéa MacLeod

Chapter 8

Hale chose a sandwich shop in a slightly better part of town from where Kitty lived. There was a phone box outside, so I quickly rang Chaz.

"I need to visit this club," I told him, quickly running down what Hale and I had found out. "Are you up for it?"

"You know I am, love. We should talk to your aunt first, though."

"Why?"

"Because she knows nearly everything that goes on in this town. And what she doesn't know, Louise does.

Maybe they'll have more background on this place. If we're going undercover, we should be prepared."

He was right. "Fine, but I've got an appointment." I would tell him about Hale later, but right now I didn't need him sticking his nose in.

"I'll ring them then. Let you know what I find out."

"Fantastic. Goodbye, darling."

The sandwich shop was a relaxed sort of place with linoleum floors, simple chairs and tables, and a menu of about half a dozen sandwiches. One could also order a pot of tea and some rather dry-looking scones. I stuck with a basic egg with cress, as it seemed the least likely to muck up.

For the first few minutes, there was an awkward silence as we ate our sandwiches and sipped slightly watery tea. Finally, I'd had enough.

"You wanted to talk. So here we are. Talk." It came out a little more abruptly than I intended, but I wasn't interested in playing games or beating about the bush.

He sighed and set down his sandwich. "I need you to know that since the day we met, there hasn't been anyone else. Not for me."

That surprised me somehow. "Truly?"

"Truly. I know our worlds are... different. Maybe unworkable. I don't know. But I only ever wanted you. From that first night, you were it for me."

"Until your past reared its ugly head," I said dryly.

"Yeah. There's that. And I can't promise it won't happen again. I haven't exactly been a priest."

Nor had I, but he didn't need to know that. "What is it that you want, Hale?"

"I want you, Ophelia." His gaze on me was intense. I could almost feel his need like a palpable thing. I shivered with the weight of it. "That's all I want. Whatever we decide this is going to be, that's what I want. Nothing and no one else."

"Then why didn't you call me when you left Dottie?"

"I wanted to be free, truly free, first. I needed to make it right. What do you say, doll?"

I swallowed hard. "I want to be with you, too. I just..."

His expression tightened. "You just what?"

"I don't know what we *can* be. I don't want marriage. Not again."

He shrugged. "Marriage is just words on a paper. What we have, no paper can define that. No legal bull can make it stronger or weaker. We are what we decide we are. Together."

I felt a little woozy inside. All sort of melty and weak. I didn't like it. Not the weakness. But I liked the melty wooziness. It felt like the best sort of whiskey, all warming and rich. I wanted to say yes, and yet I wasn't sure if I was ready to risk my heart again. He'd already crushed it once.

Being married to Felix had been light and fun. There was no heart involved in it. Merely affection and companionship. When he died, I had been sad, but in the way one is when one loses a family member, not perhaps in the way one should be when losing a spouse. But when Hale had left…

I never wanted to feel that way again. I knew I had a choice. I could live safely and never have to feel anything remotely like that again, or I could live extravagantly, loudly, and risk all the pain of all the emotions a person feels when they love with abandon.

And there it was.

I loved Hale Davis. It was that simple and that complicated. And while I may not wish for marriage and all the baggage that came along with that, I did want him.

"Well," he prodded.

"Hale Davis, will you make a dishonest woman of me?"

His smile was one of joy and relief. "I thought you'd never ask."

It was three hours later when I woke in my own bed, the afternoon sun so low in the sky the room was nearly dark. I stretched languidly and smiled to myself.

My reunion with Hale had gone rather well. He'd left an hour ago for band practice. I didn't mind. It had given me time for a quick nap before I met with Chaz. Maddie had promised to wake me up when he rang, but she hadn't. I frowned at the clock. Nearly four. What was taking so long?

I threw on my dressing gown, slid my feet into a pair of slippers, and made my way downstairs to find Maddie. She was nowhere to be seen, but my sitting room was full. Apparently, while I slept, Chaz, Aunt Butty, and Louise had put in an appearance.

"There you are," Aunt Butty called from her place near the fire where she was contentedly sipping on some sort of bright green alcoholic concoction. "Whatever are you wearing? Surely you're not greeting guests in your nightclothes."

"What are you doing here?" I demanded, ignoring her dig about my clothing. She was one to talk. Her mustard yellow dress was covered in moss green polka dots and was enough to make a person's stomach turn.

"I rang earlier," Chaz said, toasting me with his martini. "Told Maddie we were popping over for tea. Louise has some information for us."

I sank down on the divan next to Chaz. "She didn't tell me."

"Good help is so hard to find these days," Louise said in her usual loud voice. "All the young girls want to be secretaries and marry their bosses. Ridiculous nonsense. I blame Hollywood."

"Of course you do," I muttered. Chaz nearly choked on his cocktail. I ignored him, and said aloud, "What sort of information do you have for us, Louise?"

"Let the poor woman have her tea first," Aunt Butty said. "Maddie should be here any minute."

"Oh, dear." I dreaded to see what Maddie would come up with for tea. The kitchen wasn't exactly her area of expertise, although she made a fine slice of toast and her hot chocolate was excellent.

Just then, Maddie banged through the door with a wheeled tea cart I hadn't even realized I owned. On it sat two steaming pots of tea, an enormous mound of tea sandwiches, and what looked like an entire pack of Bourbon cream biscuits. As teas went, it wasn't exactly top notch, but I was pleasantly surprised she'd managed to come up with something passable.

"Sorry, m'lady," she muttered as she set out the tea things. "I meant to wake you up, but Mr. Chaz threw me off with his... shenanigans." She gave him a grimace to which he laughed.

"Maddie, my love, you are a treasure."

She sniffed. "You, Mr. Chaz, are a pain in the backside." She marched from the room, ignoring his bellow of laughter, used to his antics by now.

While I poured tea, the others helped themselves to sandwiches and Bourbons. Louise munched contentedly on a salmon paste. I'd no idea where Maddie had got that nasty stuff from, but clearly Louise was enjoying it. Occasionally she fed little nibbles to Peaches who was curled by her feet. I was glad to see he was none the worse for wear after his French adventures.

"Now," Louise said in her braying voice, "about the Apollyon."

"Yes," I said eagerly. "What do you know?"

"It's not a place a lady goes." She eyed me carefully.

"Which is why we're going under cover," Chaz said, selecting another Bourbon.

"Very well. But you should be most careful. According to my sources, Apollyon is owned by one Derby Jones."

Chaz stared at her with his mouth open. Aunt Butty let out a gasp.

"Who is Derby Jones, and why have I never heard of him?" I asked.

"Probably a good thing you haven't," Louise said dryly. "He's a gangster, my dear. Not at all our sort of person."

Since up until I married Lord Rample I hadn't been considered "our sort of person," I ignored that. I couldn't, however, ignore the reference to his status as a gangster.

"What makes you think he is involved in the underworld?"

"My dear, everyone knows it," Louise said, helping herself to a second salmon paste. I hoped she ate them all, because otherwise I'd be forced to throw them out. "His father went to prison for forging legal documents. His mother was, well, a woman of ill repute. It's well known that Apollyon is a front for laundering the money Jones makes through less-than-legal means."

"What sort of means, exactly?" I asked.

"Prostitution, extortion, you name it," Chaz said. "He's not the sort of person you want to tangle with, love."

"I don't want to tangle with him," I said. "I merely want to ask a few questions."

Aunt Butty snorted. "I'd be careful what sort of questions you ask, or you'll end up at the bottom of the Thames."

"Thank you for your concern," I said tartly, "but I think I can manage. He's a man, after all."

Chaz lifted a brow. "Which means what, exactly?"

"Which means that most men, excepting you, darling, can be led around by their, ah…"

"Yes, we know what you mean, Ophelia," Louise said. "And it's true. Especially of men like Derby Jones. But he has a type."

I groaned. "Let me guess. Rail thin with short skirts."

"You got the short skirts right," she said. "Jones, however, likes them voluptuous and tarty."

"I think she's got the voluptuous down," Chaz said.

"Unfortunately, I don't think I have anything tarty in my wardrobe," I mused.

"Oh, don't worry about that," Aunt Butty said around a mouthful of Bourbon cream. "I'm sure we can find something in my attic."

I repressed a groan. I'd no doubt my aunt had something suitably tarty, but it was more than likely a good thirty years out of date.

"How's Maddie with a sewing needle?" Chaz whispered, coming to the same conclusion.

"Passable." I hoped. Because if we didn't pull this off, no doubt Derby Jones would have us sleeping with the eels.

Chapter 9

"I do look quite the tart, don't I?" I said, admiring myself in the mirror.

"Yes, m'lady," Maddie said dryly. "Very tarty, if I do say so myself."

"It's all thanks to you," I applauded.

"And Lady Butty," she reminded me.

After tea, Aunt Butty and Louise had gone off to sort through Aunt Butty's attic. They'd returned an hour later with a pile of gowns—decades out of date as I'd suspected—and instructions for Maddie. Somehow, my maid had managed to whip up something suitable for the evening's undercover adventures.

The dress, such as it was, had been repurposed from one of Aunt Butty's red velvet gowns. It hugged my curves to the point of indecency, revealed a rather generous amount of cleavage—which Maddie had helped along with the use of a great deal of padding despite my not needing any assistance in that department—and showed rather more leg than I was strictly comfortable with. She'd also put on my makeup with a heavy hand. The end result was that instead of a lady, I looked like, well, a tart.

"Bravo," Chaz said when he saw me. "Darling, you look a treat."

"A rather cheap one," I said in a snide tone. "You think he'll fall for it?"

"If he doesn't, believe me, he doesn't bat for your team."

I snorted. "Shall we get on with it?"

We took his car, which was only slightly less flashy than mine, and parked a couple blocks away from the club. We were supposed to be ordinary folk, and ordinary folk did not drive around in expensive motorcars.

The club was located at the edge of the East End, tucked among dozens of restaurants, shops, and other clubs. It was loud, flashy, and very obvious. Inside, big band music played while women in costumes even tartier than mine strolled around serving drinks and selling cigarettes. A familiar *dastar* in the far corner caught my eye.

"Is that—?"

"Mr. Singh," Chaz confirmed. "Aunt Butty thought we could use some backup."

Mr. Singh was Aunt Butty's Sikh butler. She'd picked him up somewhere along her travels, just as she had her dreadful maid, Flora, and her new driver, Simon Vale. Mr. Singh knew things that no proper butler should know and had skills no proper butler should have. He was very mysterious, our Mr. Singh, and I liked him immensely.

He sat quietly, nursing what appeared to be a whiskey, neat, watching the crowd with what I was sure was feigned boredom. Boredom was not an expression Mr. Singh ever bore. His gaze swept over us, completely blank, as if he'd never seen us before.

"Let's mingle," Chaz said, pulling me into the crowd.

We'd formed a plan on the drive over. He and I would drink and dance and behave just as two people on a night out should behave. Once we spotted Derby Jones, I would arrange an "accidental" meeting during which I would work my feminine wiles. Once he was under my spell, so to speak, I would proceed to extract information about Dottie Lancaster Davis. Meanwhile, Chaz would work the crowd, trying to get whatever he could out of the patrons and employees. And, apparently, Mr. Singh would be watching our backs the entire time. His presence made me feel much better about the whole thing, I must say.

We found a table not far from Mr. Singh where we could keep a good eye out. Chaz got us a couple of drinks, very cheap liquor, very watered down. Then we danced a bit to the subpar band, before chatting up the people around us. No one seemed to know Dottie, and Derby Jones was nowhere in sight.

At last I visited the rather dodgy cloakroom. It smelled dreadfully of mold and unmentionable things. As I checked my makeup, a young woman came in. I recognized her as one of the cigarette girls.

"Hey, you work here?" I asked, reverting to the country accent of my youth. It was easier than trying to fake an East End one, and no one would catch me out because of it.

"Sure, doll," she said, chomping on a wad of gum. "Ya need somethin'?"

"Actually, I'm looking for a friend of mine used to hang out here. Haven't seen her in a while. Dottie?"

Her eyes, thickly rimmed in kohl, widened. "You mean Dottie Davis? Didn't you hear? Someone done her in."

I gasped in feigned shock. "No! What happened?"

"They found her in Hyde Park a couple mornings ago. Somebody stabbed her through the heart with a sword!"

Well, she was half right. "Oh, no! That's dreadful! Why would someone do that?"

"Probably messed with the wrong husband, you know what I mean?" She gave me a once over. "Don't tell me she didn't try it on with your fella. He's a looker."

I realized she meant Chaz. "She's not his type. Wasn't, I mean."

The girl snorted. "Dottie was everyone's type. At least for a good roll in the sack."

"Did you hear who killed her?"

"That husband of hers. They arrested him, but they let him go. Then they arrested some uppity lady. She got out, too. Rich always do."

"Don't they just?" I murmured.

"Don't know who they suspect now."

"What about..." I leaned close enough I caught a cloying whiff of her cheap perfume. "What about your boss?"

"Mr. Jones? I doubt it were him. He didn't care much for her." She swiped a finger under her eyes to smarten up her makeup. "Mind you, he's a dangerous man, Mr. Jones, but long as you don't cross him everything's fine. And Dottie was smart enough not to cross him." She frowned. "At least I think she was."

As I exited the ladies' room, I was eager to get back to Chaz and tell him what I'd found out, but my way was blocked by a gorilla of a man. His cheap suit jacket strained against a thick chest and shoulders wide enough to block the hall.

"Pardon me," I said, trying to move around him, but he stepped over to block me. I glanced up to find cold, dead eyes staring at me from an emotionless face. My stomach turned.

"Mr. Jones would like to see you."

I admit to some trepidation as the beefy gentleman in the too-tight suit led me through the maze-like warren of narrow hallways that made up the back of the Apollyon. Chaz had no idea where I was, and I had no idea how to find my way out of this mess. What if Derby Jones discovered who I really was and decided to do away with me? Or worse. What if he thought I really was a tart?

Frankly, I was beginning to think this had been a terrible idea. Who'd thought this caper up, anyway?

Oh, yes. Me.

With an inward sigh, I straightened my shoulders, steeled my spine, and marched on. To the gallows, as it were.

At last I was ushered into what I could only assume was the inner sanctum. It looked like any number of studies I'd seen in any number of upper-class houses. Dark wood paneling. Plush armchairs in dark wine velvet to match the drapes. Carpeting thick enough to break an ankle. And a massive rosewood desk behind which sat one Derby Jones.

Aunt Butty had shown me a picture of him in the paper before we left the house. He'd been accused of one crime or another though it hadn't seemed to stick. He was handsome in a brutal sort of way with a strong jaw, a nose that had been broken once or twice, a scar across his upper lip, and surprisingly thick eyelashes. He eyed me, his eyes the icy blue-green of the ocean. It made me shiver in trepidation, though I was fairly certain I didn't show it.

"Mr. Jones, I presume?" I said saucily in my broad country accent.

He stared at me a beat longer, then inclined his head. He didn't get up, as a gentleman should when a lady entered the room, but sat, fingers steepled, eyeing me up and down. "I am. And to whom do I have the pleasure?"

I propped a hand on one hip and eyed him back measure for measure. If he thought he could stare at me like a side of beef, well, I could do the same. He wasn't exactly hard on the eyes, either, though he was no Hale.

"Maddie," I said, giving him my maid's name. She'd no doubt throw a teacup at my head if she found out.

One eyebrow went up. "Just Maddie? No last name?" He didn't look at me like a man who was thinking of getting my clothes off.

I shrugged and took a seat in one of the velvet chairs. They actually weren't as comfortable as they looked. "What's the point? You're not interested."

"You're right."

I was surprised he admitted it.

"What I am interested in is why you're questioning my people."

My people. As if he owned them. Maybe in a way he did. Men like him bought and sold people all the time in one way or another.

"I'm trying to find out about my friend, Dottie. I know she used to spend time here." Only a partial lie. Lies are always better when they carry a grain of truth.

"And?" Those cold, appraising eyes never left my face. Not since that first perusal of my body. I almost wished he'd look somewhere else. Anywhere else. It was unnerving.

"Well, she's dead. Somebody killed her."

His expression remained impassive. No hint of surprise. "And you think someone at my club killed her." It wasn't a question.

"Honestly? I don't know. It could have been her husband or her boyfriend or that awful Kitty person," I said, ticking off random suspects. Hale might be innocent, but Derby Jones maybe didn't know that. "I was hoping maybe I could find something out here. Something that would point me in the right direction."

"Why don't you leave it to the police?"

I snorted in a very unladylike fashion. "Please. How many times have the police arrested you?"

"Fair point." He actually cracked a smile and went from brutally handsome, to downright charming.

No wonder women swooned over him. I'd never understood why women liked bad men until that moment.

Clearing my throat, I crossed my legs, something Lady Rample would never do, but something that Maddie the Tart probably would. "I know she was cheating on her husband." I knew no such thing, but I figured a person like Dottie must have been. She'd stolen her best friend's boyfriend, after all. "I'm trying to find out who it was and thought someone might have seen her here with him."

"And why do you want to find this man, if he exists?" Jones asked.

"Because maybe he knows something. Or maybe he killed her."

"He didn't." His tone was very sure.

"How do you know that?" I demanded.

"Because I was Dottie's lover."

Chapter 10

"Well knock me over with a feather," I finally managed. How had Louise been so wrong about Jones's type? I was now regretting my word choice. I didn't think Derby Jones was the sort of man to take being accused of murder very well.

"You seem surprised," he said. "Don't you think Dottie would find me... desirable?"

The way he said that last word gave me a shiver. I had a terrible feeling he might be trying to seduce me.

"Actually, I thought it might be the other way around. I've heard you have a type."

"Oh, I do." This time he did get up. He slowly stalked around the desk until he stood right behind me. His hands came up to rest lightly on my shoulders, thumbs caressing the soft skin of my throat.

A shiver went through me as I imagined those big hands wrapping themselves around my neck and squeezing the life out of me. I'd no doubt Mr. Jones could kill easily and without compunction should he decide it was necessary. Had he thought it necessary to murder Dottie?

"You do?" I managed not to squeak, but only just.

"Ah, yes. I like a woman who is strong. Independent. Beautiful." His hands slid down my bare shoulders. "One who isn't afraid of her beauty."

In other words, one who didn't mind showing off the goods. Definitely fit Dottie. But independent? That didn't. Dottie had been the sort desperate to get her claws into any man she could.

His hands slid all the way to my elbows. I was afraid I'd have to slap those hands off me, but I didn't want to stop him from whatever admission he was about to make.

Because I was sure he was about to say something important.

"I can see why Dottie fell for you," I said a little breathily.

"Unfortunately, she wasn't woman enough to handle me. Even before her untimely death." This time his face was pressed awfully close to mine. So close, I could smell cinnamon on his breath. Which was surprising. I'd expected smoke or booze. "Are *you* woman enough to handle me?"

I held back a smirk. He'd no idea. "How do I know you didn't kill her?"

"I could swear it to you."

"Would you be lying?"

"I would never lie to such a beautiful woman."

I almost burst out laughing. Laying it on just a bit thick there. "Then tell me the truth."

"Very well." His lips were inches away from my jaw. "Dottie and I were lovers for a time. It was brief. Casual. And then we both moved on. I did not kill her. Had no reason to."

And there it was. He'd have killed her if he'd felt there was a reason. No doubt about it. But he, surprisingly enough, seemed to be telling the truth.

"Now, let's talk about you and me." His voice was low and sultry. Filled with dark promises.

I stood up so fast, he staggered backward. I turned to face him and gave him a cool, accessing look. "I'm very flattered, Mr. Jones, but I'm afraid you're not my type."

And I sashayed from the room, leaving the man gaping behind me.

It took three tries to find my way back to the club. Without Derby Jones's goon to show the way, I kept getting lost. One time I ended up in the men's room. Fortunately, it had been sans men at the time. Another time I nearly locked myself in a closet. But at last I found the chaos of the dance floor.

I careened across the crowded space until I found Chaz. Grabbing him by the sleeve, I dragged him toward the door. "Come on. We'd better go before he changes his mind."

"Until who changes his mind?" he shouted over the music.

"Derby Jones."

His eyes goggled. "You met Jones?"

"Hurry. I'll tell you all about it once we're outside."

Out of the corner of my eye, Mr. Singh rose from his table. As we passed the bar, I noticed the barman staring at us. The look on his face was equal parts fear and suspicion. Very strange. Still, I didn't have time to mull it over. For all I knew, Derby's goon was already on his way.

After collecting our coats from the coat check girl, we exited the club. It was late, and the streets were empty. A light drizzle frizzed out my wave and dampened my shoes.

"Now tell me—"

"In the car." I hustled him faster.

We were halfway down the block when the club door banged open and someone shouted, "You there!"

I couldn't be sure if it was the goon or Jones, but either way, I didn't want to stop for a chat. Instead I shouted, "Run!"

We ran full tilt for the car, leather soles slapping on pavement, echoing off the walls of the brick buildings surrounding us. Behind us I heard a shout, but I didn't dare turn around to look.

Chaz was ahead of me. He yanked open the car door and held out a hand. Too late. Somebody grabbed me from behind, fingers sinking into the soft flesh of my upper arm.

I tried to yank my arm free, but to no avail. Lifting cocktails does not exactly give a person a lot of muscle tone. Instead, I trod on my attacker's instep with my heel. He let out a yelp, and his fingers loosened. I whirled around and bashed him over the head with my handbag. He hit the deck like a ton of bricks.

Unfortunately, a second goon loomed close, glowering fiercely as he jumped over his fallen comrade. However, Mr. Singh melted out of the darkness, landing a fist on the man's jaw.

Without further ado, I ran for the car and jumped inside. Chaz slammed the door behind me and dashed around to his own side of the car. "Go! Go! Go!"

Needed no urging. I revved the engine and gunned it. The car took off with a lurch and screech of tires. A quick glance in the rearview mirror showed both goons on the ground. Mr. Singh had disappeared.

"Mr. Singh to the rescue. What the devil did you hit that other goon with?" Chaz asked, hanging on to the strap.

"Aunt Butty insisted I put a brick in my bag," I said.

"You're kidding." He grabbed my bag, pulled it open, and peeked inside. "No brick."

"Of course not. I didn't have a brick. But I figured a book would do just as well."

He pulled out a fat tome upon which was written in gold letters *The Complete Works of Shakespeare*. "You mean this book?"

I grinned. "That's the one."

"You'll be lucky if you haven't killed him."

"Well," I sniffed, "he shouldn't go around grabbing ladies. He only got his just desserts."

But as we zoomed into the night, I couldn't help glancing in the rearview mirror from time to time, keeping an eye out for goons. The roads remain clear, or at least as clear as they ever got in London, but I had a bad feeling it would only be a matter of time before Derby Jones was on my tail.

Chapter 11

Once our pursuers were well out of sight, I rounded the block and headed back toward the club.

"What are you doing?" Chaz demanded. "They'll see us."

"No, they won't. They'll think we're long gone."

"So what's the plan?" he asked as I parked the car halfway down the block with the bonnet pointed at the club.

"The barman," I said. "He knows something. I'm sure of it. The club will be closing soon, so we'll wait here until he comes out."

"And then what? Kidnap him?"

"Don't be ridiculous." Though the thought had crossed my mind. "We're just going to pull him aside and question him. I have a feeling he'll tell us a lot more if he knows his boss isn't watching."

"I doubt he'll tell us anything at all," Chaz groused. "You don't cross Derby Jones. Not if you like your limbs intact and working."

Great. Not only had Jones sent his goons after me, but he probably considered what I'd done crossing him. If he found out who I really was, he'd probably break my shins. Or worse. But I couldn't think of that now. I needed to focus on clearing my name.

It was late. I was cold. And I'd give anything for a drink. Sans that option, I could use a snack. I rummaged around in my handbag for some mints or something but came up empty.

"Open the glove box door," I ordered.

Chaz sighed, but did as told.

"Anything of interest?"

He shuffled things around. "Road map. Extra pair of driving gloves. And a nearly empty tin of boiled sweets." He rattled it.

"Give it over." I pried off the lid and popped a sweet in my mouth. I offered him one, but he shook his head.

"You think Jones is behind Dottie's death?" Chaz asked.

"I don't know," I admitted. "He's definitely capable of killing someone, but the manner of her death doesn't seem his style. Probably more likely to shoot someone or drop them in the Thames. Stabbing someone with a woman's hatpin seems... unlikely."

"Did he admit to having an affair with her?"

"Surprisingly, yes," I said.

"Why surprisingly?"

"He didn't seem the sort to just admit it. And Louise was very specific about his type. Something just felt off."

He eyed me. "You had a hunch."

"Yes, I did."

He sighed. "And now I get to freeze my nether regions off, waiting on a barman who may or may not know something interesting."

"Buck up," I cheered him. "It's not everyone who gets the chance at a stakeout."

"North would have a fit if he knew what you were up to."

"Let him." I crunched the last of the boiled sweet and selected another. "If I leave it up to him, I'll be hanging from the gallows in no time."

"Don't be dramatic, love. They don't hang ladies. At worst you'll end up in Bedlam."

"Lovely," I said dryly. "I could use a holiday."

The doors of the club swung open, and patrons spilled out onto the street, some staggering, likely from copious amounts of cheap alcohol. Finally, the last one left and the light above the door switched off.

"He'll have to clean up," I said, "but it shouldn't be long now."

About twenty minutes later, the door opened again, and the barman exited the building and strolled toward us. His head was down, hunched against the cold, hands jammed in his pockets.

As he drew even with us, Chaz swung open the door and stepped out onto the curb right in front of him. The barman muttered something—either an apology or curse, it was hard to tell—and started to go 'round him. Only Chaz grabbed his arm. "We need to talk." He shoved the poor man in the backseat of my car before he could protest.

"Whatcha want?" he demanded, staring at us with wide, frightened eyes.

"We ain't gonna hurt you," Chaz said in a rather unconvincing rough accent, "*if* you tell us what we want."

"What do you want? Who are you?"

I turned around, and he got a good look at my face.

"Oh, it's you." He seemed to relax at least a little.

"I saw you inside," I told him. "It looked like you wanted to tell me something."

"I saw you talking to Mr. Jones," he said. "You know him?"

I shook my head. "No, but I knew Dottie Hale." A little white lie. "I wanted to know if he knew what happened to her. He said he didn't. Claimed they were lovers."

The barman snorted. "There weren't no love lost between those two."

"Why do you say that, er, what's your name?" Chaz asked.

"Harry."

"Nice to meet you, Harry. I'm... Maddie," I said, once again giving him my maid's name. "And this is my partner, Jimmy." Seemed like a good name for a tough.

"Right. Well, trust me when I say Mr. Jones weren't havin' relations with the likes of Dottie Hale."

"How can you be sure?" I asked.

"Well, she were a regular weren't she? Came in nearly every day. Drank a bit. Flirted with this one or that one. Sometimes got real close, if you know what I mean."

Chaz and I exchanged glances. We did know.

"Jones don't touch the likes of that no how. If he's with a woman, she better not be with anybody else, you get my drift?"

"We do," Chaz assured him.

"Why would Jones lie to me then?" I mused. "He claimed they were lovers."

Harry snorted. "Opposite of that, more like."

"What do you mean?" I asked.

He leaned forward. "If Mr. Jones finds out I told ya, he'll kill me."

"He won't find out," Chaz assured him.

"You didn't hear this from me," Harry said, "but that Dottie stole money from Mr. Jones. He were that furious, he swore he'd get her."

"Get her?" I had a bad feeling I knew exactly what Derby Jones had meant by that.

Harry nodded. "If you ask me, Derby Jones killed Dottie Hale."

It didn't surprise me to find someone accusing Derby Jones of murder. In fact, I was quite certain he was capable of just such a thing. Question was, was he guilty of this particular murder?

The most interesting tidbit was that while Derby had claimed to be having a relationship with Dottie, the barman had been quite certain he was doing no such thing. In my experience, barmen tend to know things about both their employers and patrons that other people simply don't. They're rather like butlers in that regard.

There was nothing more for it but to go home and get some rest. I dropped Chaz off at his flat, then tooled home to my own townhouse. Maddie was still abed, so I made myself a cup of tea, then sequestered myself in my room. It wasn't long before I'd nodded off.

I'd no idea how long it was later, though it felt like but a minute or two, when pounding on the front door woke me from a deep sleep. The pounding was followed by

Maddie's screech and a lot of shouting, then feet thumping on the stairs. This did not bode well.

Jumping from bed, I threw on a robe and slippers, then flung open the door and shouted in my most imperious lady-of-the-manor voice, "What the devil is going on!"

The hall was crowded with people. Maddie stood in front of my bedroom door, one hand braced against the frame as if to bar the way. Facing her was Detective Inspector North in all his glory, bushy eyebrows beetled angrily. Behind him ranged several uniformed coppers. One even had his billy club out.

"Someone tell me this instant what is going on," I demanded.

"I will not let them take you, m'lady," Maddie assured me, rather dramatically, I thought.

"Hush, Maddie. Detective Inspector North, I demand to know what's going on."

He straightened his shoulders and eyed my nightwear, blushing slightly. "Lady Rample, you are under arrest for the murder of Harry Simpel."

I blinked. "Harry whom?"

North gritted his teeth. "The barman at Apollyon."

"Harry's dead?" The last time I'd seen him, he'd been hale and hearty, although terrified Jones would find out he'd ratted on him. Had Jones found out Harry talked?

"You know very well he is," North snapped. "Stabbed him through the heart with a hatpin, just like Dottie Hale."

"Don't be ridiculous." I was suddenly worried about Chaz. He'd been with me when we talked to Harry. If North found out, he might accuse Chaz of murder, too. Worse, if the killer knew…

He stepped forward. "I'm afraid you'll have to come with us."

I sighed. "May I get dressed at least?"

"Sorry. Can't have a murderer running loose, can I?"

I gave him a cold smile. "You will hear from my solicitor."

"Be that as it may—"

"Maddie," I shouted over him. "Call my solicitor. Then ring my aunt."

North blanched. "I'll give you five minutes."

Shéa MacLeod

Chapter 12

I was ushered once again into the same jail cell. The officer on duty appeared a bit embarrassed and offered me an extra pillow and blanket, which I gratefully accepted. North had also allowed me to bring a book to entertain myself, though I was far too keyed up to actually read. It was more a power play on my part. I wanted to let him know he didn't frighten me one whit.

Granted, the thought of sitting in jail wasn't a comfortable one. I'd been hoping I could find the real killer before this happened. Instead, the killer had struck again and in such a way as to make me look guilty. Rather clever that.

There was no doubt in my mind that Derby Jones was, indeed, the killer. Who else would murder poor Harry? I could think of no other reason he would be murdered unless his death was connected with Dottie's.

Indeed, our other suspects—Archie and Kitty—were in no way connected with the club that I could see and had no reason to kill Harry. The only way I could see that Harry and Dottie were connected was through the club and one Derby Jones.

It was sometime after lunch—vile fish paste sandwiches and lukewarm weak tea—when the door to the jail opened and Aunt Butty came sailing in. She wore a pale pink gown with far too many ribbons and ruffles and an enormous pink hat that barely fit through the doorway.

"There you are, Ophelia." Her footsteps clacked against the stone floor. "I told North he was being ridiculous. He didn't take it well."

"No, I imagine he didn't," I said dryly as she paused in front of my cell. "How is Chaz?"

"Fine, the dear boy, though quite in a rage over you being arrested. He told North he was with you when you spoke to Harry, but North refused to arrest him as he had an alibi for the time of death."

"I'm surprised North didn't throw him in jail for being an accessory."

"He threatened it, but he has no proof. I really detest that smug little man," Aunt Butty said.

She and I were of one mind there. "Have you spoken to Louise?"

"Yes, and Varant. I'm afraid there's no getting you out this time."

I sighed. "I was afraid of that."

"I won't stop trying," she assured me. "In the meantime, I brought you a basket of goodies which the on-duty sergeant said he has to search. Both our gazes went to the sergeant who started guiltily. "I assured him I know exactly what is in that basket, and none of it had better be missing when it comes to you."

"I'm sure he'll make sure I get the basket intact," I said, trying to play the politician.

"What should I do, Ophelia?" Aunt Butty asked, suddenly looking worried.

The fact Aunt Butty was worried made my stomach a bit queasy, but I stiffened my spine. All was not lost just yet. "Talk to Chaz. Maybe between the two of you, you can figure out a clue to help prove my innocence."

She nodded. "Already on it. We're having a confab at my flat this afternoon. Tea, cakes, and investigations. We should start our own club." She brightened. "Actually, it's a marvelous idea."

"Yes. Grand. While you're at it, tell Chaz I'm certain Derby Jones is the killer." I quickly explained my reasoning.

She nodded, her massive hat wobbling dangerously. Her poor hatpins were getting quite the workout. "Makes absolute sense. I'll have a word with the boy. And what about Hale?"

"Let him know what happened, and tell him about Jones and Dottie. Maybe he'll have some ideas." I wished like anything I could see Hale just then. He'd a way of making me feel better about things.

Just then, the sergeant cleared his throat, indicating our time was up.

"Chin up, Ophelia. What doesn't kill us!" And with that, Aunt Butty sailed from the room, and I was left alone to ponder my current situation.

The sergeant appeared with my basket of goodies. "Cheer up, milady. Things can only get better."

I snorted as I accepted the basket. "I'll cheer up when I prove my innocence and rub North's face in it."

He grinned as if the thought cheered him no end. "There's the spirit!"

If only I felt so confident.

The night passed with intolerable slowness. The cot was hard, the blanket thin, and the cell cold. Around midnight, they brought in a drunk who proceeded to spend the rest of the wee morning hours singing rather bawdy drinking songs. What was with this place and singing drunkards?

"Would you please be quiet," I shouted at last. "Some people are trying to sleep."

To which he began shouting out "Brother John" quite loudly and off key. There was nothing left to do but join him. At least until the guard arrived and shouted at us both to shut up. After that, the drunk mumbled softly to himself.

He finally fell asleep around four in the morning. I knew because the snoring was loud enough to rattle the bars.

At last I gave up on getting any sleep and instead paced the cell, trying to keep warm. I'd give anything for a highball right about then. Or better yet, a hot toddy, heavy on the whiskey. This being arrested for murder nonsense was getting old.

By seven, the sun was streaming through the narrow window set high in the stone wall. It was a welcome sight, as my stomach had been rumbling for half an hour. Surely breakfast was nigh.

At eight, the morning on-duty sergeant appeared with a covered tray. I sniffed the aroma of bacon and tea appreciatively.

I ate to the dulcet tones of snoring. The bacon was under cooked and greasy, the toast a bit scorched, the eggs rubbery, and the tea weak. I skipped the milk as it smelled a bit off. Still, beggars can't be choosers, so I ate everything with relish.

Feeling more the thing, I fixed my hair best I could and tried to smooth the wrinkles out of my dress. At least North had let me put clothes on and not marched me to the station in my night things. Although I might have been more comfortable if he had.

It was nine on the dot when the sergeant reappeared, shoving his key in the lock of my cell and turning it with the grate of metal-on-metal. He swung open the door.

"What's this?" I asked.

"North is letting you go," he said.

I squinted suspiciously. "Why? Where is North?"

"He ain't here, Mrs. Rample. Er, I mean milady." He flushed, though I'm not sure his embarrassment was from improperly addressing me or having to tell me North wasn't available.

I gave him a cool look. "Why am I being released?"

"No idea. I was told to let you out, so I'm letting you out."

"Very good." I stepped out of the cell with something like relief and followed him away from the snoring.

I hadn't brought anything with me save the clothes on my back and my book, so he led me straight to the front desk. There in the lobby sat Aunt Butty dressed dramatically in a black gown and matching hat, all trimmed in purple. Even the feathers on the hat were purple, the massive plumes waving wildly every time someone pushed through the front doors.

"Ophelia!" She jumped to her feet and rushed to mash me against her bosom.

I hugged her back a moment before setting her a bit away from me. Mostly so I could breathe. "Why did North let me out?"

"I'm unsure. I got a call this morning to come collect you. That's all I know."

I frowned. "The sergeant didn't know either." The idea that no one seemed to know why I'd been set loose on the populace concerned me. After all, I was supposed to be a dastardly murderer. "Something has happened, I'll bet."

Aunt Butty blinked. "What do you think it is?"

"No idea. If only North were here." I sighed. "I'll tell you what, though. We should visit the morgue."

"The morgue?" She repressed a shiver. "Why ever for? You do know the morgue is full of dead bodies, don't you?"

"The morgue also contains the medical examiner. I want to know what he knows about the murders of Dottie and Harry."

"Very well," Aunt Butty said. "We shall visit the morgue, but none of those bodies better move."

I was in full agreement with her on that point.

Chapter 13

It had taken a great deal of persuasion on my part—and a little bit of threatening on Aunt Butty's—but we finally got the details of the morgue where Dottie and Harry had both been sent. It was but a short walk from the station, so we braced ourselves against the chill morning air and stepped out.

It was one of those drizzly sorts of mornings so common in London, but fortunately for us, Aunt Butty had her enormous brolly to hand. She put it up immediately and we both huddled beneath as we strode down the walk.

The morgue was in a rather non-descript building which also housed the local hospital. Naturally it was in the basement, as things that people would rather forget about often are.

We passed a young man in a white suit wheeling a gurney down the hall. On it rested a lump covered in a sheet. I decided to pretend I didn't know what it was.

"Young man," Aunt Butty said imperiously, "we need to speak with the coroner at once."

"H-he's in his office," he stammered, pointing down the hall. Apparently, he wasn't used to aristocrats storming the castle, so to speak.

"Very good." And Aunt Butty sailed on.

I followed in her wake, leaving the poor fellow shaking his head behind him. He'd still be wondering what hit him a year from now.

The coroner's office was clearly marked with a brass plaque: M. Mortimer, Coroner.

"Rather unfortunate name," Aunt Butty mused. "It rhymes in a most repulsive manner." She rapped on the door with the handle of her umbrella, then shoved open the door without waiting for an answer.

M. Mortimer, Coroner, sat behind his desk, staring at us through round tortoise shell glasses. It was hard to tell how tall he was, but he was very round with a fringe of graying hair surrounding a shiny bald pate. He wore a goatee—very out of vogue—and was in his shirtsleeves. A white lab coat hung from a coat stand in the corner.

"Pardon me," he said, half rising. "Who are you, and what are you doing in my office?"

"I am Lady Lucas," my aunt announced before I could open my mouth. "And this is my niece, Ophelia, Lady Rample."

If the coroner was surprised to have two such auspicious persons in his office, he did not show it. "And?"

"And we are here about some murders," she declared.

That was when I decided to step in before he rang the police on us. I did not need North changing his mind and stuffing me in a cell again. "A dear friend of mine was killed recently. Dottie Hale. Stabbed. Very sad."

His eyes widened. "The hatpin through the heart?" His suspicions were clearly not allayed. "You were friends with her?"

"My niece has friends in many places," Aunt Butty assured him. Her inference being that I had friends in very high places indeed, not just the lows dwelt by such as Dottie Hale.

"Er, well, I'm sorry for your loss," he said somewhat lamely.

"Thank you. I am given to understand that recently there was another, quite similar, murder."

That surprised him. "There was indeed. A man this time. Also stabbed through the heart with a hatpin."

"Was he found in a park like dear Dottie?" Aunt Butty asked. Personally, I thought she was laying it on a bit thick.

"No. He was found in an alleyway near his flat."

Which meant the park wasn't the connection.

"Odd thing was—"

We both stared at him. "Yes?"

"The hatpin he was stabbed with? It was an exact match to the one that killed Mrs. Hale."

"A heart shaped hatpin?" I almost whispered.

He nodded. "That's the one. With lots of little jewels on it. Fake, of course, but pretty. Nothing like the third victim."

"Third victim?" I managed. Was that why North had let me go?

"The dead woman they found this morning." He picked up a clipboard and squinted at something. "One Katherine "Kitty" Leonard."

Aunt Butty and I both gasped, staring at each other with wide eyes. Kitty was dead?

"What happened?" I finally managed.

"Looks like they found in her Hyde Park not far from where they found Mrs. Davis," the coroner continued. "She was stabbed with something other than a hatpin."

My heart sank. "It couldn't be the same killer then, could it?" And if it wasn't the same killer, then why had North let me go? I wouldn't have thought him that stupid.

"The hatpin was added later," he continued, "but that doesn't mean it wasn't the same killer. Hard to tell sometimes with these things. The hatpin alone is a good indicator the deaths are related, don't you think?"

Aunt Butty and I gaped at him, but he didn't notice. He just stared at the clipboard.

"Interesting. The pin was heart shaped like the other two. Killer's a right cupid, isn't he?"

"Astonishing," Aunt Butty managed as we exited the morgue. She was not wrong.

"I guess that explains why North let me go," I said. "The murders were obviously committed by the same person, and I have an alibi for Kitty's death, so..."

"They're not necessarily the same person," Aunt Butty pointed out what I was already worried about. "Kitty's death was different. The hatpin was added later and was not the murder weapon."

"If North decides to arrest me again, please don't mention that," I said dryly. "Although there could be any number of reasons the actual murder was committed with a different weapon."

"Like what?"

"Perhaps Kitty was suspicious, on guard, unlike the others. She was able to fight back, and he had to stab her with something else... a knife, perhaps. But he brought the pin with him, obviously, so he left his calling card, just like with the others." Which meant the killings had been planned, not just a spur-of-the-moment thing. Then again, with multiple murders, the whole passion killing defense was out the window.

"Or someone else killed her and made it look like it was the same killer. Or the first killer decided to take advantage of her murder by someone else by sticking in the hatpin."

"I admit the first is possible," I said. "But the second option seems a bit unlikely."

"It would rely on a fair amount of coincidences," Aunt Butty agreed. "Still, it's possible, and North is just the sort of man to glom on to such a thing."

Again, she wasn't wrong. Unfortunately. "I still think it's the same killer. I mean, who else would have three matching heart shaped hat pins?"

"Someone who really likes hearts?"

I rolled my eyes. "No, this cupid killer had this planned all along, I'm betting."

"Do you suppose it's a mass murderer like Jack the Ripper or Mary Ann Cotton?" She looked positively giddy at the thought.

"Maybe," I mused. "But based on the relationship of the victims, I'm betting that it's someone who has a very specific purpose in murdering these people but wants to make it *look* like there's a mass murderer on the loose."

"Perhaps if we look more closely at the victims, we will find our killer. Obviously, Kitty and Dottie were friends at one time and Harry knew Dottie from the Apollyon."

"And Dottie and Harry both knew and worked with Derby Jones," I pointed out.

"Did Kitty know Mr. Jones?" Aunt Butty wondered as we climbed into the car and I started the motor.

"Good question. We should go have a look at Kitty's place. I have a feeling she knew more than she was letting on," I said. I pulled into traffic to much blaring of horns and barreled down the road heedless of pedestrians.

Kitty's flat proved to be a short drive from the morgue. Before we knew it, we were pulling up to the rather dilapidated building. I was nervous about leaving my car alone. "Perhaps you should stay here," I suggested.

"Nonsense." Aunt Butty strode down the pavement to where a couple of lads were playing some sort of game with tin cans. "You there!" They stared at her. I could imagine how things must have looked from their angle. "I will give you each one of these," she waved a coin at them, "if you guard that motorcar," she stabbed a finger in the direction of my vehicle, "with your lives. When I return there had better not be a scratch on it." And without waiting for an answer, she whirled around and marched back toward me.

"How do you know they'll do it and not just steal my tires?"

"Trust me." There was a glint in her eye. "They'll do it." I'd no doubt those boys had seen the same glint and that they'd do exactly what Aunt Butty told them to.

"Very well," I sighed. "Let's go."

"Are you sure the place will be empty?" Aunt Butty puffed up the rickety stairs behind me. I kept having visions of the treads giving way and us plunging to our deaths.

"Not totally," I admitted. "She said she lived with her current boyfriend, but hopefully he won't be at home."

He wasn't. No one answered our knock. It was but a matter of a minute or two before I had the lock picked and we were standing inside Kitty's flat.

It looked very much like it had the day I'd visited previously. The sink was full of dirty dishes, underclothes were strung on a line to dry, and the place smelled of dust and rotting foot.

Aunt Butty wrinkled her nose. "Appalling. How will we find anything in this mess?"

"Very carefully. Why don't you look around in here and I'll search the bedroom?"

"Fine with me. Based on the state of this room, I don't want to see what the bedroom looks like," she said.

The flat was one of those horrible places that didn't have its own loo. One had to jaunt down the hall in one's nightclothes and hope one's neighbor wasn't taking his own sweet time. I was very glad I didn't have to live in such a place.

The only room other than the kitchen area was the bedroom which was just big enough for a double bed. There wasn't even space for a wardrobe or nightstand. Instead, there were pegs along the wall from which hung numerous dresses, cardigans, cheap purses, and overcoats of varying thicknesses. Shoes were thrown haphazardly under the bed.

A shelf had been nailed to the wall on one side of the bed and appeared to serve as a sort of dressing table. There was a small mirror, a bottle of drugstore perfume, a chipped glass containing a couple of well-worn lipsticks, a box of powder, and a couple pots of inexpensive face creams. There was also a hatpin cushion, currently containing a single cheap enamel hatpin, its head in the shape of a flower. Which didn't mean anything. I didn't know a single woman who didn't own at least one hatpin.

What there wasn't was any sign of a man living there. I found that very odd, seeing as how Kitty had claimed to live with her new beau.

Perhaps he'd split once he heard she'd died. Only there was no indication of that being the case as the pegs were all full. I would have thought he'd have at least used one, which would now stand empty. And there was no space for male footwear beneath the bed, nor any sign any had been there. The only empty space was just large enough for a single pair of shoes. No doubt the ones Kitty had been wearing when she was killed.

Which left one option. Kitty had lied about the boyfriend. Either she had one, but he didn't live with her, or she didn't have a boyfriend at all.

Option one made little sense. If she had a boyfriend, why would she lie about him living with her? I could see her lying about such a thing to Dottie, wanting to make it appear as if she was over her betrayal, but to two perfect strangers? There would be nothing in it for her.

Option two, on the other hand, made a lot of sense if she were trying to divert suspicion. If she had a boyfriend and was happy in her new life, she'd have no reason to harm Dottie in revenge for stealing Archie. However, if she didn't have a boyfriend and was still pining for her lost love, killing Dottie suddenly became a real possibility.

Except for one thing. The murderer had killed three people, and Kitty had hardly done herself in. No, I was still betting on Derby Jones.

I took a last look around, checking every pocket and even under the pillows. Nothing. So I knelt on the threadbare rug and began turning over shoes. I only had three left when a bit of paper fluttered out of one. It landed on the floor face down.

Dropping the shoe, I scooped up the bit of paper and turned it over. It was a photograph of Dottie and Kitty standing together in front of the Natural History Museum. Both had wide smiles on their faces. Kitty's eyes sparkled with laughter while Dottie... well, someone had drawn a slash of red lipstick right through Dottie's face.

Chapter 14

Later that evening, Chaz, Hale, and I gathered at Aunt Butty's flat to review our findings so far. When Hale arrived, I beat Mr. Singh to the door and dragged Hale into the tiny box room Aunt Butty claimed was a "study" but was really more of a nap room. It was nice to have a moment to ourselves before rejoining the madness that was our lives.

Over boulevardiers, which Chaz mixed up despite Mr. Singh's protestations that cocktails were *his* purview, we discussed the facts of the case so far. Including my and Aunt

Butty's trip to Kitty's. I told them about finding the photo and my conclusions about Kitty's lies, along with my realization that she couldn't be the murderer anyway.

"And what about you, Aunt B," Chaz drawled. "What did you find?"

"Precious little. There was a biscuit tin with a few shillings and a receipt from a pawnbroker for a men's pocket watch."

"Probably stolen," Hale said dryly.

"Maybe from the mysterious boyfriend of whom no one can find hide nor hair," Chaz suggested, taking a long swallow of his cocktail.

"So we are at an impasse," I said with a sigh. The idea made me melancholy. If I couldn't find the real killer, and soon, I'd no doubt North would find an excuse to lock me up again.

"Buck up," Hale said softly, running a finger down my bare arm, resulting in a shiver. "Things will come out all right. They always do."

He had a point. Things had seemed very dark after he'd left France to marry Dottie. I'd been sure that was it. I would never see him again. And now, here he was.

I felt the tiniest stab of guilt. I shouldn't be so glad a woman was dead. No one deserved that. Not even the terrible Dottie. But she *had* used her lies to steal Hale away, and that was unforgiveable. If you've got to lie to get or keep your man, there is something intrinsically wrong with your relationship to my mind.

Of course, I reminded myself, Dottie wasn't like me. I had enough money I didn't need a man. But a woman like Dottie... she'd probably felt she had no choice. That she needed a man to make her way in the world. Still, she could have easily found someone else, not lied about a pregnancy to get her way. I couldn't say I was entirely sorry she was gone.

I dragged my attention back to what Aunt Butty was saying. "—of course, what we need to do is get into Derby Jones's office."

"Oh, no." Chaz sat bolt upright. "The two of you should stay away from Jones. He's dangerous. We already found that out. Look what he did to poor Harry."

Poor Harry, indeed. Stabbed through the heart with a hatpin. Ghastly. And all he'd done was tell us the truth. That is, if him spilling the beans was the reason he'd been killed, which I assumed it was. What other reason could there be?

"We don't know for sure that Jones killed Harry." I played devil's advocate. "It *could* have been someone else."

Hale gave me a look. "You don't believe that."

I sighed. "No, I don't. But there's only one way we're ever going to prove anything."

"I agree," said Aunt Butty, swinging one leg over the other as she drained the last of her cocktail. "North is useless. We have to do this ourselves."

"There's safety in numbers," Hale pointed out. "How about you all come see my band perform tonight. Then afterward, we'll see about digging the dirt on this Mr. Jones."

"Are you sure?" I asked. Hale didn't often go on our little adventures with us, usually because he was busy performing.

"Hey, I've got as much stake in this as you do."

True. It was his wife who'd been killed, estranged or not. And if he felt for me even a fraction of what I felt for him, my being charged with murder wouldn't go down easily. "All right, it's a plan."

Chaz groaned. "Overruled again."

Aunt Butty snorted. "Amusing, seeing as how you're usually the one up to your eyeballs in Ophelia's shenanigans."

"Maybe we should bring Mr. Singh along, too," I said, eyeing Aunt Butty's mysterious butler who was currently mixing up more cocktails.

He bowed elegantly. "I live to serve."

"What about your chauffeur, Simon Vale?" Chaz suggested. "He was in the army, wasn't he?"

"Wonderful idea, dear boy," Aunt Butty approved.

That meant there were six of us against Derby Jones and whatever goons he had with him. Hopefully it wouldn't matter, and we'd be able to sneak in and out without him noticing. Facing Mr. Jones was simply not on the agenda.

Aunt Butty clapped her hands in delight. "Let the first investigation of our murder club commence."

I groaned. "I think we need a better name."

The Lion Club was much as I remembered it from my failed date with Varant. I felt a little pang over the fact I hadn't seen or spoken to him recently. I hadn't had much of a chance to thank him for getting me out of jail the first time.

It wasn't the sort of pang one feels over losing a loved one. But more a pang of relieved guilt when one is about to get out of an awkward entanglement. While I thought Varant was rather dishy and was often useful to my "little adventures," as Aunt Butty called them, the thought of becoming Lady Varant made me squeamish. And Varant was not the sort of man to accept any arrangement other than marriage.

I wondered if he'd be terribly upset with me, or if he, too, would be relieved. It was hard to say with Varant. He was a bit of an enigma.

Shoving thoughts of Varant aside, I focused on the energy in the room. The band was playing a zippy number, Hale really pounding away at those ivories. Aunt Butty was on cocktail number three, her foot tapping along to the beat as dancing couples swirled around us. Chaz was chatting up a sultry young man at the bar, while Mr. Singh was outside with the car. He'd insisted that such an upscale establishment was no place for a butler.

It was late—or early, depending on how one looked at it—and exhaustion pressed heavily on me. I'd had a very long day after an even longer and sleepless night. I wanted nothing more than to be tucked into my warm bed, with the promise of hot cocoa in the morning.

Instead, I'd donned a rather simple black evening dress, a pair of matching t-straps, and a single pearl strand necklace. While I'm no Aunt Butty, the outfit was boring even by my standards. It was, however, perfect for a night of breaking and entering.

We waited until last call was announced by an elegant gentleman in a black tuxedo, before gathering our coats and exiting the building. Aunt Butty's chauffeur, Simon, brought the car around. Mr. Singh sat next to him looking somber. I hoped he wasn't upset about our asking him to join us. I'd seen Mr. Singh in a crisis before, and the man was astonishingly steadfast and a quick thinker. Just the sort of person you'd want with you on a crime spree.

We piled in the back and Simon motored around to the back entrance where we waited for Hale to put in an appearance. About twenty minutes later, he finally did, much to our relief. The car was a bit chilly, despite the valiant efforts of the heater and multiple layers of clothing.

He popped in beside me and wrapped his arm around my shoulders. "All right, boys and girls, are we ready to commit a felony?" he asked as Simon pulled away from the curb.

"Hardly that," Aunt Butty sniffed. "We've no intention of stealing anything, and therefore it's simply trespass. A civil matter at most."

"You English sure do have a different way of looking at things," he said easily.

A few minutes later, Simon stopped the car in an alleyway a few blocks from Jones's club. The place was narrow and stank of rotted garbage and stale urine, but it was the perfect location to conceal a vehicle as obvious as Aunt Butty's bright red 1929 Rolls Royce Phantom.

We all clambered out, and this time Mr. Singh joined us. Only Simon stayed behind to guard the car and enjoy a cigarette. I didn't smoke and found the habit vile, but for once I almost wished I was staying behind with him. Instead, I girded my loins and joined the others on the pavement.

We found a good spot where we could keep an eye on the Apollyon but could remain unseen by anyone exiting the building. The club was dark, which unfortunately meant nothing. Based on previous experience, they shut the light off shortly after last call to avoid an influx of drunks looking for a new drinking hole. Shortly after that, they'd kick out their inebriated patrons, and shortly after that, the employees would exit out the back door. Based on my watch, the employees should be leaving right about now.

Sure enough, the back door banged open, and half a dozen people sauntered out. Their voices carried on the chill night air. They strolled by us, smoking and chatting about events of the evening and who was doing what after getting some sleep before they splintered off in various directions, disappearing into the night.

"I didn't see Jones," Chaz muttered. "Or his goons."

"Nor did I," I said. "Maybe he wasn't there tonight."

Hale snorted. "Unlikely. Word on the street is he never misses a night. Likes to keep a tight rein on things."

"Makes sense," Aunt Butty said. "After all, if your ill-gotten gains were tied up in such a business, wouldn't you want to keep an eagle eye out?"

"You got that right," Hale agreed.

"What do we do then?" I asked no one in particular. "How do we get Derby Jones and his goons out of the building? If they're even in there."

"Carefully," Chaz muttered.

I made a face at him. "Don't be an ass."

"I could go knock on the door," Aunt Butty suggested. "Tell them I'm lost."

Hale shook his head. "They'll never believe you. You're not exactly the sort of person that usually hangs out in this part of town."

"I suggest we wait for one hour," Mr. Singh spoke up at last. "It is unlikely that Mr. Jones would stay longer than that. It should be sufficient time for him to count the night's takings and mark them in his books. Once that is done, he will most likely be on his way and we will be able to enter without incident."

It was the most amount of words I'd ever heard him utter at once, and naturally it was the most logical suggestion. So we waited. Meanwhile, my toes grew numb and my feet turned to blocks of ice. I was beginning to wish I'd worn my fur-lined boots. Why hadn't I thought of that? They would have been out of place in The Lion's Club, of course, but I could have kept them in the car and worn them for our investigation. I refused to call it breaking and entering. It wasn't. While it may be trespass, it was for a good cause.

And if North bought that, I had a bucket of sand to sell him.

At last, the back door banged open and a hulking, gorilla-like shadow appeared. As he moved into the light cast by a nearby streetlamp, I realized it was one of Jones's goons. He stopped on the pavement, looked right and left, then turned and gestured.

A moment later, Derby Jones and Goon Number Two joined him. They were all heavily muffled in thick, wool trenches, knitted scarves, and bowler hats pulled low over their brows, but their builds and features were nonetheless unmistakable.

"We should probably wait a few," Chaz suggested. "Make sure they don't come back."

The minutes ticked intolerably on. At last, when it had been five minutes, I gave up. "Come on. Let's go. We can't stand here all night." And without waiting for an answer, I strode across the street.

Shéa MacLeod

Chapter 15

Naturally, the alley door was locked. No surprise there.

"I could pick it," Chaz said. "Might take a while."

"What about the window?" I assumed it led to a cloakroom.

Hale squinted up at it. It was set high in the wall. "Not sure any of us could reach it. Not unless you've learned to fly recently."

I snorted. "Don't be a ninny. One of you can hoist me up."

Hale and Chaz exchanged glances.

I propped my hands on my hips. "I'm not that heavy."

"No, my lady, you are not," Mr. Singh said. "I am certain I could lift you easily."

I gave the boys my haughtiest Lady of the Manor look. *There. Take that.*

"However," Mr. Singh continued, "the window is quite small. I don't know that you will fit."

"Of course, I will! Easy peasy. Come on then." I waved him closer to the brick wall and hoisted my skirt.

"Oh, dear," Aunt Butty murmured.

"This is not going to go well," Chaz muttered.

"Oh, ye of little faith," I said. "Right, then, Mr. Singh. Ready when you are."

Before I knew it, I was practically flying through the air as Mr. Singh heaved me toward the window. I caught the ledge with my fingers and shoved at the sash. It slid up quite easily. Huzzah!

"A little higher, Mr. Singh," I shouted down.

He shoved me higher, high enough I could fling my arms up and over the ledge, hoisting myself up to my armpits. However, that was as far as I got. I hadn't the arm strength to pull myself higher, and Mr. Singh had already lifted me as high as he could manage. I wriggled a bit, trying to get further up, but it was no use. Beside which, my shoulders were wedged at an angle in the window. It was too narrow. At least it wasn't my hips, I suppose.

Though the room was too dark to see inside, from the smell it was definitely a cloakroom. I wrinkled my nose, turned my head, and shouted, "I can't get in."

Chaz snorted.

"Don't be crass," Aunt Butty said. I heard the *thwap* of her handbag, no doubt against the back of his head.

"Not to worry, Ophelia," Hale called up. "Chaz has the lock open."

"What?" I shrieked, still clinging to the window sill. "I went through all this for nothing?"

There was a telling silence.

I sighed deeply. "I really need new partners in crime. Very well. Mr. Singh, please help me down."

"Of course, my lady. Please pardon my impertinence."

"Your what?" But before I could ask for further clarification, his hands gripped my thighs rather higher than was decent for a man who was neither husband nor lover.

Mr. Singh pulled on my legs, but I didn't budge. "Let go, my lady."

"I have let go."

He tried again, but my shoulders were firmly wedged into the window. The only result was that one of my garter straps gave way, and my right stocking drooped a bit before sliding down my leg to flop in poor Mr. Singh's face.

"Oh, dear. Sorry about that, Mr. Singh," I called down.

"No worries, my lady."

Behind him, the others snickered.

"You better watch yourselves," I threatened. "When I get down from here—"

"How about I go inside and help push from the other side," Hale suggested. Quite as if I were a jacket potato stuck in an oven.

"Jolly good," Chaz said brightly. "I'll keep watch."

"I'll just bet you will," I grumbled.

"What's that, dear?" Aunt Butty called up.

"Nothing."

A few moments later, the light in the room came on—it was indeed a cloakroom, and not a particularly nice one—and Hale appeared. He flipped the lid down and climbed up on the commode, his face now level with mine.

"You have got yourself in a bit of a pickle, haven't you?"

"Rather," I said dryly.

"It's your coat," he said, peering closely at my shoulders. "The thick fabric has got you wedged in pretty good."

It was nice of him to blame the fabric, and I told him so. His answer was a quick peck.

"Now I'm going to shove you from this side. It'll be at an angle, and it may hurt."

"Do what you must," I told him.

"Ready, Mr. Singh?" he shouted.

"Ready, sir," came Mr. Singh's muffled reply.

"One!" Hale said loudly. "Two. Three. And shove!"

And shove, he did. While Hale pushed at my shoulders, Mr. Singh gripped my thighs and tugged downward. My upper arms scraped against the window frame hard enough to leave bruises, and I popped clear of the window, sailing backward to land right in Mr. Singh's arms.

He set me carefully on the ground before turning his back, so I could fix my garter. Ever the gentleman, Mr. Singh.

"Good heavens, Ophelia," my aunt said, striding to check me head to toe. "You do like to get yourself in the oddest situations."

I would very much have liked to say it wasn't my fault, but I *had* been the one who'd insisted on trying to climb through that blasted window. Instead, I said, "Yes, Aunt, I do rather."

"Now come along. We've a hotbed of iniquity to search." And Aunt Butty strode away, leaving me and Mr. Singh to follow in her wake.

By then, Chaz had got the lights on and was already combing through the main bar area. Hale came out of the cloakroom, wiping his hands on his handkerchief.

"That room's clear." He winked at me. "Mr. Singh and I can check the storage rooms."

I nodded and waved to my aunt to follow me. "Jones's office is this way."

She trotted behind me down the same narrow halls the goon had taken me. They were dimly lit and somewhat musty.

Finally, we came to the door behind which stood Jones's office. Naturally, it was locked.

"Too bad there's no window," Aunt Butty said dryly.

I gave her a dirty look. "I know a few tricks." I pulled a pin from my hair and went to work on the lock.

I was not as efficient as Chaz, but I finally got it open and we stood in the inner sanctum of a gangster. It gave me something of a chill.

It must have had the same effect on Aunt Butty, for she said, "Let's hurry so we can get out of here."

While I rifled through his desk, Aunt Butty searched the file cabinet. At last we both stood back with matching expressions of exasperation. The only thing of interest either of us found were a set of books for the revenue man, but only one set.

"Nothing," she said. "That is preposterous. The man is as dirty as the Thames."

Which was very dirty indeed. "Where else would he keep secret documents or murder weapons?"

She tapped her chin with one red nail. "I recently read about a man who kept a secret safe."

I lifted a brow. "You read about this?"

She stiffened. "Yes. In *The Wily Detective* by Dexter Dodge."

"Sounds American."

"He is. He writes marvelous detective stories. Although I've a feeling Dodge is really a woman using a pseudonym."

"Why?" I couldn't believe I was asking.

"Because the mysteries are far too ingenious to have been written by a man."

Of course, they were. I pinched the bridge of my nose. "Aunt Butty, that is a work of fiction."

"Fiction is often based on fact," she said. "And Jones is just the sort of criminal to have a secret safe. Quickly, look behind the paintings and such. I am certain it's here."

I shook my head, but did as she commanded, lifting the frames of the half dozen paintings and photographs scattered about the walls. They were in need of a good dusting, but otherwise, were unremarkable. "Nothing here."

"Under the desk then." She pointed.

"Ugh." But, naturally, I dropped to my knees and pawed around under the desk, nearly knocking myself unconscious when I clipped my head on the edge on the way out. "Nope."

She tapped her chin again, eyes narrowed in thought. Then she began to pace the room. It wasn't the sort of pacing people do when they are bored or thinking or irritated. No, it was a very deliberate sort of pacing and every once in a while, she'd stop and sort of press her foot to the floor.

"You're looking for loose floorboards," I said.

"Naturally. Since there aren't any bookshelves, it's the only other option."

"Bookshelves would stand out a bit in here," I agreed before joining her in her pacing.

We'd been at it for a few minutes when Aunt Butty shouted, "Ah ha!" She pressed a section of the floor and it squeaked and shifted beneath her foot.

I hurried over and knelt down. The floorboard, hidden under the edge of the rug, was definitely loose. I used a metal nail file from my handbag to pry it up. Beneath was a safe. It looked to be made of cast iron and had a combination dial on the front.

"Oh, dear. I don't suppose you can pick that?" Aunt Butty said with a frown.

"Unfortunately, no. I don't think Chaz can either."

"I may be able to help," Mr. Singh said softly from the doorway.

I nearly keeled over in fright. I hadn't heard him come up the hall. The man moved like a cat.

"Have at it." I climbed to my feet, allowing him access to the safe.

"I will need absolute silence, my ladies," he said gravely.

We both nodded solemnly.

Mr. Singh knelt beside the safe and leaned down until his ear was nearly upon it. Then he began to fiddle with the dial. It seemed to take an interminable amount of time, but at last there was a slight popping sound, and he swung the door open. Rising to his feet, he gestured toward the gaping safe.

We scrambled forward and peered inside.

Aunt Butty's eyes widened. "Oh, my."

For there, nestled inside, was a second set of books.

"So, Derby Jones really is a crook," Hale said later that night, or rather, earlier that morning, back in my sitting room.

We'd escaped the Apollyon unscathed, both sets of books in hand. After dropping Chaz off at his place, Simon had let us off at mine before taking Mr. Singh and Aunt Butty home. I'd kept hold of the books. After all, it was I who'd taken my husband's properties and holdings and turned them from a nice, steady income to something wildly successful. I knew all about keeping books. Even a simple perusal proved that Derby Jones was, as Aunt Butty had claimed, dirty as the Thames.

"Yes, he is," I said, looking up from the pages I'd been comparing. "He's definitely laundering money through the club. See, this first set of books which we found in the file cabinet is for the revenue man. He's making a very nice profit." I tapped the second set. "These are the real figures. He's clearing tens of thousands more than he should be, and it's all coming from sources other than the club."

"Definitely money laundering, then." Hale perched beside me. "Can you tell specifically where it's coming from?"

"Maybe. It'll take some more digging as it's all in code, but I'll bet my last farthing it's all illegal."

He reached over and massaged my shoulders. I nearly moaned with delight.

"Aren't you worried Jones will discover you've taken the books?" he asked.

"I've no doubt he will notice first thing in the morning that *someone* has taken them, but I don't see how he'll know it's us." At least, I was hoping he wouldn't know. I dreaded to think what would happen if he figured it out.

"Will you take those to the police?"

I nodded. "Once I figure out how this ties into the murders."

"Are you sure it does?"

I rubbed my forehead. "It has to."

"Come, my love. You've been at this long enough and it's nearly morning. Let's go to bed."

Sounded like a good offer to me. I trailed him up the stairs, but it took forever to fall asleep and even when I did, my dreams were filled with numbers, hatpins, and Derby Jones's disturbing laughter.

Chapter 16

The next morning, with still no clue as to how to prove Derby the killer, I decided what I needed was a good head-clearing. And the best way to clear one's head, I always think, is a trip to Harrod's. Some may disagree with me, but some just enjoy being disagreeable.

Since I'd not slept well, I was up and about unusually early and arrived at the front doors of the distinguished department store at precisely ten in the morning. I made a beeline for the handbags but couldn't find any that suited me. I was about to move on to the shoe department, when I quite literally ran into Binky.

Binky is really Alphonse, the new Lord Rample, but everyone calls him Binky for reasons entirely unknown to me. He was my Felix's cousin many times removed and inherited the title and a crumbling manor house in the wilds of darkest North Yorkshire simply for being the last man standing, as it were. I got the rest of the lot, something for which he has never really forgiven me.

"Hullo, cousin, fancy seeing you here," he said, once I'd righted myself.

I didn't correct him. It was no use. Binky insisted on claiming relation. I think he was under the impression he'd get Felix's money when I kicked off. If that was the case, he would be sorely disappointed. He was a bit of a worm and not the sort of person I typically cavorted with. However, there was a rather young handsome woman by his side, and I found myself curious. Women frequently flung themselves at Binky due do his title and the fact he liked to pretend he wasn't flat broke.

"Ah, Ophelia, this is my cousin on my mother's side, Philoma Dearling. Phil, this is Felix's wife." He sighed. "Ophelia, Lady Rample."

"You can call me Ophelia," I said. "All my friends do."

"Oh, lovely. Call me Phil."

Phil was charming with dark hair and big, blue eyes, her lithe figure wrapped in a smart, auberge dress that looked rather delightful on her but would have looked ghastly on me. Her jewelry was Egyptian revival and looked rather smashing. Aunt Butty would have loved it.

"I'm staying with Phil in town while I have some work done on the roof," Binky explained, no doubt lying through his teeth. We both knew the roof wasn't getting fixed any time soon.

"I've a lovely little mews house not far from here," she explained. "Not much room, but we muddle along, don't we Binky?"

Binky made a harrumphing sound, no doubt embarrassed he was forced to rely on the kindness of his cousin. I ignored him. "Why don't you join me for tea?" I suggested instead. "I could use a cuppa."

"Delightful! Come along, Binky." And she strode away toward the tea room.

"I like her," I told Binky as we followed along.

He grunted. Very manly of him.

Over a pot of Assam and an assortment of cakes, Phil and I chatted about our lives in London. Turned out, she had been living in Paris the last few years, studying art.

"Marvelous fun," she said, nibbling on a ginger biscuit. "Parties every night with all sorts of lovely cocktails and famous people. One night I had a good snog with Scott Fitzgerald. I mean, I didn't know it was him until later. Well, I knew it was him, but I didn't know who he was. A married man, too. What a cad." But she didn't seem terribly upset by it.

"You should come to one of my aunt's parties," I told her. "You'd enjoy them immensely. That's precisely the sort of thing she loves to throw... all sorts of artists and bohemian types. The odd Hollywood director or whatnot. Just all sorts. She once had a trapeze artist visit and perform in the sitting room. It was wonderful until the trapeze fell and tore out a chunk of ceiling plaster. The artist was fine, of course… a little banged up. Nothing a shot of whiskey couldn't cure. But it took Aunt Butty ages to fix that ceiling."

We were on our way out when we passed a display of hatpins. Suddenly my brain started buzzing. Ideas flitted in and out, zipping around like bees.

"Oh!"

"What is it?" Phil asked.

"I think I know what happened." And I charged out the door.

Behind me I heard Binky tell a startled Phil, "Don't worry. She gets like this. Likely she's up to her eyeballs in murder again."

I drove straight to the morgue and marched inside, ignoring the stares of its denizens. Not that there were many... alert enough to stare, but I definitely got a few looks from the white-suited orderlies as my heels tapped against the marble floor.

I found the medical examiner in the middle of an autopsy and had to back out of the room quickly as my tea threated to put in a second appearance. I waited impatiently in the hall until he was able to join me.

At last, his round figure appeared in the doorway. "Ah, Lady Whatsis."

"Rample."

"Indeed. To what do I owe the pleasure?" He trundled down the hall, and I followed.

"Remember when my aunt and I spoke with you about the murders?"

He nodded. "The Cupid Murders."

"Is that what they're calling them?"

"Well, North is," he admitted.

"Ghastly man. That's appalling. He really shouldn't give murderers such chirpy names."

"You're telling me. Now what can I do for you, Lady Rample?"

"The hatpins. The ones the killer used. What did they look like?" I asked.

He frowned. "I told you before. Heart shaped."

"Yes. You said the first two were heart shaped and covered in little paste jewels."

"That's right." He tucked his hands behind his back and rocked on his heels. "Lovely little enamel and paste things. Made to look expensive."

"Though not actually so?"

He shrugged. "Not really up on ladies' hatpins, but I wouldn't have thought so, no."

"What about the third one?"

"Oh, well, that was different. Also heart shaped and enameled, but the enamel was chipped and there were no jewels."

"Not a matching pin then?"

"Most definitely not," he assured me. "Although the basics were the same, of course. No doubt the first were a pair and he, or she, got whatever else they could get their hands on that was close."

"Anything else unusual about them?"

He started to shake his head then paused. "Well, there was something about the third one. Something different from the first two."

My heart beat faster. "Yes?"

"It had something on it. On the head. As if the killer had something on his hands."

"What sort of something?" I could hardly breathe with excitement.

"Dark-colored grease."

I took the front steps to the police station as quickly as I could. I wished I'd worn trousers, so I could take them two at a time, but alas, my skirt was too confining, and I could not. By the time I reached the top, I was huffing and puffing, and my feet were starting to feel a bit pinched.

I shoved my way inside, nearly toppling a lady of the evening who was trying to exit. She gave me a rude gesture which I ignored. Not because it was beneath me—I've no problem giving as good as I get—but because I was too focused on my mission.

"North!" I all but shouted at the poor desk sergeant.

He stared at me with wide eyes. "Er, Mrs. Rample. I mean, Lady Rample. DI North ain't here. I mean, he left earlier. I mean, he's gone to lunch." He stammered out the words like he was terrified I might pummel him.

I narrowed my eyes and leaned over the counter. "Where's he gone?"

The sergeant's cheeks flushed crimson, and he stuttered some more. "I r-really couldn't say, my lady."

"Is that so?" I infused my voice with levels of Aunt Butty I never knew I had.

"He's at the sarnie shop down the road," he blurted, pointing wildly.

"Why, thank you, sergeant. Too kind." And I tossed the end of my scarf over my shoulder, adjusted my hat, twirled semi-elegantly around, and sashayed out the door. It would have been a magnificent exit if the end of my scarf hadn't got caught in the door and nearly strangled me to death. The poor sergeant had to come to my rescue.

Once freed, I hurried down the pavement in search of the sandwich shop. It was halfway down the block, tucked between a tobacconist and a tailor specializing in men's clothing alterations. North was sitting in the window, newspaper in one hand and sandwich in the other.

I rapped on the window and when he looked up, gave a little finger wave. He grimaced and looked away, but he couldn't deter me. I entered the premises as if I owned the joint, ignoring the stares of the working-class patrons, and strolled right up to North's table.

"Mind if I sit?" I didn't wait for an answer but draped myself in the chair in as elegant a fashion as I could muster. The place stank of overcooked eggs and fish paste mixed with the odor of men who tended to sweat for a living. Don't even get me started on the clouds of cheap cigarette smoke that threatened to choke me near to death.

"What do you want?" North snarled, rattling his paper in a meaningful fashion.

I eyed him carefully, enjoying every moment of this, my victory. "I know who the Cupid Killer is."

He snorted. "Don't you think you've gone a tad too far this time?"

"Not at all. I have *proof*."

He set both his sandwich and his paper down. "What proof?"

I wagged a finger at him. "Now. Now. All in good time." I slid a piece of paper across the table.

He glared at it. "What's that?"

"A list of names."

"And what am I expected to do with it?"

I gave him my most winning smile. "Tomorrow, gather together the people on that list and take them to the address at the bottom. All will be revealed." And despite his protests, I rose and exited the building feeling quite smug and sure of myself as I drove home.

After parking the car, I headed up the walk, going over in my mind my exact plan for the next day. It would be very exciting, and I would prove to that dratted North that when it came to detecting work, I knew what I was doing.

I was about to open my front door when someone grabbed me from behind and rammed a hood over my head.

I tried to scream, but he clapped a hand over my mouth, dragged me back down the walk, and pitched me into a waiting motorcar!

Shéa MacLeod

Chapter 17

"What do you want?" I demanded as the car careened around a corner, throwing me against what felt like a wall. There was no answer, and I lifted the hood. It was pitch black, and I could hear things rattling in the dark. I must be in the back of a delivery van.

At last the van stopped, the engine shut off, and the door slammed. Footsteps crunched in gravel as someone walked around the van and unlocked the back doors. I felt around blindly for something to use as a weapon, but it was too late. The doors swung open, and bright light blinded me.

"Get out," a snarly, masculine voice ordered. "I've got a gun, so you better do as I say."

Not wishing to be shot dead, I carefully crawled out of the van and onto an empty gravel lot. As my eyes adjusted, I realized who my captor was.

"Archie. What the devil are you doing?"

Kitty's former boyfriend didn't answer. Instead he gestured toward a dilapidated garage with his weapon. "Inside."

I didn't want to go inside, but I didn't see any alternative, so I stumbled along, trying to come up with a clever escape plan. Unfortunately, before I could drum up anything, he had me tied to a chair.

"Archie, this is madness. You must let me go."

"Shut up!" Once he had me tied up, he walked away, disappearing into another room.

The minute he was out of sight, I did two things simultaneously: I took stock of my surroundings and tried to loosen my bonds. The first was easy enough, the second, not so much.

The garage was about as expected: concrete floor stained with motor oil, random chains hanging from the rafters, loads of dust and cobwebs everywhere. It was a defunct version of the garage where I'd first met him. How would anyone ever find me here?

They wouldn't. I'd just have to take care of this myself.

He'd tied me up good and tight, but there was something he hadn't counted on: my reading proclivities. Aunt Butty had lent me the latest novel by Dexter Dodge—the same one in which she'd read about hidden safes. In it, the detective had been kidnapped by gangsters. While being tied up, he'd kept his muscles contracted so that while the kidnappers thought the bonds were tight, once he'd relaxed, there'd been some slackness in the ropes. So I'd done the same thing. And it had worked!

The ropes he'd tied me with were just loose enough I could move a bit. And, feeling around, I realized the chair on which he'd tied me had a metal frame that was rusty and rough. Just the thing. I began working away at the ropes.

Then Archie returned with a bottle of beer of all things and began pacing and muttering to himself. I'd a terrible feeling he was gearing up for something dastardly. There was nothing for it. I must distract him!

"Listen, Archie, nothing could be that bad. Surely, if you explain, everyone will understand."

He turned on me. "No! They won't. They'll hang me for sure."

"But why?" I said, playing dumb. "You're a good man. Whatever you've done, you've done for good reason, I'm certain of it."

"You don't know what I've done!"

"You killed Kitty," I said, proud of how calm I sounded, and also wondering if I'd made a mistake confronting him in this way.

He stared at me before taking a long swallow of beer. "How'd you know?"

"There was grease on the hatpin," I said simply, still working at my bonds. "Dark grease. I remember it was all over your hands when I visited your establishment."

He let out a string of expletives. "I knew I'd never get away with it."

"So why'd you kidnap me?" The ropes were very loose now.

He scrubbed a grease-stained hand through his hair. "I dunno. Seemed like a good idea at the time."

"Yes, I can see how you might think that. But really, I do believe that it would make more sense to get out of London as quickly as possible." I wriggled a hand free.

"You're a good man, Archie, anyone would understand how she drove you to it. It was her fault really."

"The coppers'll never believe it."

"But of course they will. I'll tell them. And you know they'll listen to me." Bald-faced lie, but anything to keep Archie distracted.

"You'd talk to them for me?"

"Of course. I know the lead detective on the case. We've spoken on numerous occasions." Never mind that he'd be more likely to throw me in jail than to listen to anything I had to say. My second hand was nearly free. "Listen, my throat is really dry. Could you get me something to drink?"

He grunted and disappeared into the same room as before. I yanked my hands free and the rope dropped to the floor. It was quick work to undo my ankles. I searched around for a weapon as I heard his footsteps approaching. The only thing I found was a rusty wrench.

Snagging it off a workbench, I dashed to the side of the open doorway and lifted it. As Archie stepped through, I brought it down on his head. He dropped to the floor in a heap, two open beer bottles crashing to splinters. Beer sprayed everywhere, including on me.

The doors crashed open, light streamed in, and male voices shouted, "Police! Drop your weapon!"

The wrench hit the floor and I reached for the sky.

Chapter 18

"Maddie, remind me to give you a pay raise," I said as she set the tea service in front of me.

"Yes, my lady. I'll write it in lipstick on your mirror." She had a sparkle in her eye as she stepped out the door.

As well she should. It had been Maddie who'd seen Archie take me, and Maddie who'd rung Chaz and Hale immediately. Chaz had rung Aunt Butty, who'd rung Varant, who'd told her where I was being held before ringing the police. Then Hale and Chaz had joined the police on their raid. It had all been very exciting.

After assuring me he'd stop by later, North had let the two men take me home where I'd washed off the reek of beer and changed into fresh clothes. Aunt Butty had met us there and the three of them were already deep in the liquor cabinet.

Aunt Butty whipped out a flask and dumped its entire contents into the teapot. "Medicinal."

"Of course," I murmured, enjoying the flavor of heavily doctored tea. "I assume North arrested Archie."

"Of course," Chaz said, sitting next to Aunt Butty. "Although he did admit he isn't sure why Archie should only be arrested for Kitty's murder."

Just then the doorbell rang, and Maddie's footsteps clacked along the front hall. There was a murmur of voices, more footsteps, and then North appeared in the doorway, hat in hand.

"My lady, I was just stopping by to check that you'd survived your little adventure." Was it me, or was there a hint of snark in his tone?

Aunt Butty snorted. "Of course she did. She's made of sterner stuff than that, Detective." I noted she left off the "chief inspector" portion of his title. "Now sit and have some tea. Ophelia was about to tell us why Archie should only be arrested for Kitty's murder and not the other two deaths."

"Was she now?" he muttered, taking a seat as ordered.

"Well, Archie only killed Kitty, obviously," I said, earning myself a glare from North.

"Then who killed Dottie and Harry?" Hale took his place beside me. "Were we right about Jones?"

"Afraid not. Kitty killed them," I said, taking another swallow of tea flavored whiskey.

"What?" North sputtered.

"Perhaps you should explain," Aunt Butty said.

"Right, well, according to the documents I found in Derby Jones's office—"

"Which you broke in to," North interrupted.

Chaz shoved a cup of tea and a plate of biscuits at him. Probably to try and shut him up. This was my moment in the sun, after all.

"Yes, well, be that as it may, Kitty used to work for him. And I think there may have been more going on than that as she was just Jones's type. In any case, when Dottie stole first Archie and then Derby—or at least his business—

Kitty was furious. She immediately began to plot her revenge.

"The night of the murder, she sent Dottie a message. Dottie thought it was from Derby and that he was finally going to, ah, give in to her charms. Instead, it was Kitty who met her in the park and stabbed Dottie through the heart using a hatpin from her own collection."

"Good gosh," Chaz said. "That's appalling. But what about poor Harry?"

"Kitty'd been hanging around Apollyon trying to get back into Derby's good graces when she saw us talking to Harry. Of course, Harry knew all about what had been going on and she was afraid he'd spilled the proverbial beans. So she killed him, too. And being somewhat clever, she thought she could make it look like a mass murderer was on the loose by using the same method of death and the twin to the first hatpin," I explained. "What she didn't count on was Archie realizing she'd done it. I mean he told us from the beginning it was her. And when the police didn't arrest her, he confronted her himself."

"And she admitted it?" Hale asked.

"According to Archie, yes. Told him she'd done it for them. Only Archie wasn't in love with Kitty anymore.

He was besotted with Dottie. When Kitty confessed to murdering his new obsession, he stabbed her with a screwdriver in a fit of rage."

"But what about the hatpin?" Aunt Butty asked.

"He knew he had to throw the police off the scent, so he went out to a second-hand shop and bought a cheap hatpin in the same shape and pushed it into the wound, hoping they would think it was the same killer," I said.

"He obviously doesn't understand modern forensics," Chaz said dryly.

"Ain't that the truth," North muttered around a biscuit.

"I'm just glad you're safe," Hale murmured, wrapping an arm around my shoulders.

"What about that terrible Derby Jones?" Aunt Butty wanted to know.

"With the documents the two of you found, there's enough to put Jones away for a very long time," North assured us.

"Well, that's a relief," she said, refilling her cup. "Can't have nasty pieces of work like that running amok."

"No, we cannot," North agreed, polishing off his biscuit before rising from his seat. "Well, I must be off. Do try and stay out of my way, will you?" And with that he marched out of the room.

"Fat chance," Chaz chuckled.

"Oh, Chaz," Aunt Butty said, reaching under her chair and coming up with a parcel, "I know it's a bit early, but I have your birthday gift here."

"Why, thank you, Aunt B." He grinned happily. "So kind of you."

"Wait 'til you open it," I muttered.

He ripped open the paper and froze a moment, before lifting out a mustard yellow monstrosity of a hand-knitted scarf. "Er, it's quite… something, Aunt B. Thanks awfully."

"I know the winter is nearly over," Aunt Butty said, "but there will still be plenty of cold weather for you to enjoy it."

He looked a little pale. "Can't wait."

I snickered, and he shot me a dirty look before stuffing the scarf back in the wrapping. "You know, Aunt B., you finding the secret safe was quite something. I bet Jones will be steamed when he hears about it."

As the two of them chatted about the future repercussions of Derby's enterprise being broken up, Hale leaned into me, his breath warm against my ear. "With all this talk of the future, perhaps we should talk about ours."

My heart thudded in my chest as I turned to meet his gaze. His eyes were warm and full of meaning, and I found myself in dire need of another medicinal cup of tea.

"Yes," I whispered eagerly. "Yes, I think we should have a talk."

His thumb rubbed circles on the back of my hand. "Shall I throw them out?"

I turned to glance at Aunt Butty and Chaz who were already both a little tipsy and arguing over the best way to off a wayward spouse without getting caught. I held back a smile.

"Let them argue it out. We have plenty of time to talk. I'm not going anywhere."

He gave me a long, slow, sultry smile. "Nor am I."

Shéa MacLeod

Coming in Spring 2019

Lady Rample and the Mysterious Mr. Singh

Lady Rample Mysteries – Book Seven

Sign up for updates on Lady Rample:
https://www.subscribepage.com/cozymystery

Shéa MacLeod

Note from the Author

Thank you for reading. If you enjoyed this book, I'd appreciate it if you'd help others find it so they can enjoy it too.
Lend it: This e-book is lending-enabled, so feel free to share it with your friends, readers' groups, and discussion boards.

Review it: Let other potential readers know what you liked or didn't like about the story.

Sign Up: Join in on the fun on Shéa's email list:

https://www.subscribepage.com/cozymystery
Book updates can be found at www.sheamacleod.com

Shéa MacLeod

About Shéa MacLeod

Shéa MacLeod is the author of the bestselling paranormal series, Sunwalker Saga, as well as the award nominated cozy mystery series Viola Roberts Cozy Mysteries. She has dreamed of writing novels since before she could hold a crayon. She totally blames her mother.

She resides in the leafy green hills outside Portland, Oregon where she indulges in her fondness for strong coffee, Ancient Aliens reruns, lemon curd, and dragons. She can usually be found at her desk dreaming of ways to kill people (or vampires). Fictionally speaking, of course.

Shéa MacLeod

Other books by Shéa MacLeod

Lady Rample Mysteries
Lady Rample Steps Out
Lady Rample Spies a Clue
Lady Rample and the Silver Screen
Lady Rample Sits In
Lady Rample and the Ghost of Christmas Past
Lady Rample and Cupid's Kiss
Lady Rample and the Mysterious Mr. Singh (coming Spring 2019)

Viola Roberts Cozy Mysteries
The Corpse in the Cabana
The Stiff in the Study
The Poison in the Pudding
The Body in the Bathtub
The Venom in the Valentine
The Remains in the Rectory
The Death in the Drink

Notting Hill Diaries
Kissing Frogs
Kiss Me, Chloe
Kiss Me, Stupid
Kissing Mr. Darcy

Cupcake Goddess Novelettes
Be Careful What You Wish For
Nothing Tastes As Good
Soulfully Sweet
A Stich in Time

Dragon Wars
Dragon Warrior
Dragon Lord
Dragon Goddess
Green Witch
Dragon Corps
Dragon Mage
Dragon's Angel

Shéa MacLeod

Dragon Wars- Three Complete Novels Boxed Set
Dragon Wars 2 – Three Complete Novels Boxed Set

Sunwalker Saga
Kissed by Darkness
Kissed by Fire
Kissed by Smoke
Kissed by Moonlight
Kissed by Ice
Kissed by Blood
Kissed by Destiny

Sunwalker Saga: Soulshifter Trilogy
Fearless
Haunted
Soulshifter

Sunwalker Saga: Witchblood
Spellwalker
Deathwalker
Mistwalker
Dreamwalker
Omicron ZX
Omicron Zed-X
A Rage of Angels

www.sheamacleod.com

Printed in Great Britain
by Amazon